THE MISSING DOG IS SPOTTED

THE MISSING DOG
IS SPOTTED

Jessica Scott Kerrin

Groundwood Books
House of Anansi Press
Toronto / Berkeley

Published in Canada and the USA in 2015 by Groundwood Books

Groundwood Books / House of Anansi Press
110 Spadina Avenue, Suite 801, Toronto, Ontario M5V 2K4
or c/o Publishers Group West
1700 Fourth Street, Berkeley, CA 94710

We acknowledge for their financial support of our publishing program the
Canada Council for the Arts, the Government of Canada through the Canada
Book Fund (CBF) and the Ontario Arts Council.

Canada Council   Conseil des Arts
for the Arts   du Canada

ONTARIO ARTS COUNCIL
CONSEIL DES ARTS DE L'ONTARIO
an Ontario government agency
un organisme du gouvernement de l'Ontario

Library and Archives Canada Cataloguing in Publication
Kerrin, Jessica Scott, author
The missing dog is spotted / written by Jessica Scott Kerrin.
Issued in print and electronic formats.
ISBN 978-1-55498-726-9 (bound).—ISBN 978-1-55498-728-3 (html). —
ISBN 978-1-55498-826-6 (mobi)
I. Title.
PS8621.E77M58 2015   jC813'.6   C2014-906789-5
C2014-906790-9

Cover illustration by Sam Kalda
Design by Michael Solomon

Printed and bound in Canada

To my sister, Leslie, the veterinarian

Table of Contents

One

——

Club Photo

TREVOR HATED high shelves more than anything. So he sighed deeply when he discovered that the book he wanted — *The Case of the Waylaid Water Gun* — was sandwiched between other mystery novels on the tallest bookshelf at his school's library.

Out of reach.

He searched for the rolling footstool that the librarian used from time to time. He discovered it in the next aisle and pushed it back to his spot where he wedged it against the stack so it wouldn't move. Trevor climbed up and reached.

No luck.

He stood on his tippy-toes and reached again.

Still no luck.

He stepped down and began to pile books from the lower shelf onto the stool to give himself more height.

Big thick books.

"Need some help?"

Trevor recognized the voice, a classmate.

He looked up. Way up. It was Loyola Louden.

Loyola Louden, the school giant.

For the past year, ever since Trevor had arrived at Queensview Elementary to enroll in grade six, the two of them had had a secret, unspoken pact. Under absolutely no circumstances were they to appear together side by side.

Ever.

It wasn't because they didn't like each other. They actually didn't know each other all that well. As far as Trevor could tell, Loyola was a perfectly normal grade-six girl. She hung out with a typical group of chatties, they talked nonstop about clothes, they whispered to each other by holding their hand to the other person's ear rather than just speaking under their breath like the boys did, and when they giggled, which was all the time, it was typically over nothing. To Loyola and her circle of friends, everything was a Very Big Deal.

Trevor hardly paid them any attention. But he couldn't help noticing how Loyola struggled to blend in despite her height.

Once, when the class was handing in assignments by passing their work to the person who sat in front of them and so on all the way up to the first row, Trevor spotted Loyola's handwriting. It was tiny and cramped, as if her words wanted to take up as little space as possible on the white page.

In recent months, she had also started slouching. Just a bit. Especially when she was sitting with the chatties outside of class, like during lunch. When the giggling became too much and a teacher called out to them to pipe down, she would hunch like a Galapagos tortoise pulling into its giant shell.

Also, Trevor had noticed a change in her color choice for clothes. She had moved away from the brilliant pinks and oranges that the chatties favored on the days that they didn't have to wear their school uniforms. Now she wore browns and grays and dark greens, turning herself into an invisible backdrop for the merry parade of shorter girls surrounding her.

Then there was her voice. She had started speaking in softer tones, maybe thinking that doing so somehow made her appear smaller. It didn't. Besides, her booming laughter gave her away. It filled the corners of the room and turned every head within earshot.

Trevor knew one more thing about Loyola. Whenever she met someone for the first time, it was the same routine. She was asked if she was a basketball player.

Loyola, who despised basketball, always had a great comeback.

"No," she would say. "Equestrian's my thing. I'm actually training to be a jockey."

Trevor enjoyed the next part — the confused look on the face of whoever had suggested that Loyola was a basketball player. Either they didn't get her sense of humor, or they didn't know what a jockey was.

Trevor knew all too well that jockeys were elite race-horse riders.

He also knew that the ideal jockey was small.

Unusually small.

Like Trevor.

Trevor was the shortest boy in his class. In fact, he was shorter than the boys below him in grade five.

And the boys in grade four.

And even a few in grade three.

Trevor understood exactly why Loyola didn't like standing next to him. It was because she'd look like the giant in "Jack and the Beanstalk."

Or the beanstalk.

So they stayed clear of each other, their secret pact standing between them.

"What are you doing here?" he asked.

"Borrowing books," she replied curtly, a stack of them on her hip.

Awkward silence. Then the library's telephone rang.

"Queensview Elementary Library," Ms. Wentzell, the librarian, said from behind her desk. "How can I help you?"

A short pause and then, "Oh dear. How sad," Ms. Wentzell said, her voice stricken.

Both Trevor and Loyola drifted out of the aisle and toward her desk.

"No, I haven't seen it. But I will keep a lookout. What's your telephone number, just in case?"

She jotted it down.

"And you've checked with the animal shelter? Of course. Of course. I'll ask around and I'll let you know. Bye for now."

Ms. Wentzell sadly shook her head as she hung up.

"What's wrong?" Loyola asked.

"Someone's lost a dog," she explained. She got up from her desk and went to the library's window. She looked across the school's soccer field and scanned the fence line.

"What does it look like?" Trevor asked.

"White with brown spots. Short ears. Medium-sized."

All three studied the landscape, but there were no dogs with spots mingling with the recess crowd.

"If not here, then maybe the cemetery," Ms. Wentzell suggested.

"The cemetery?!" Trevor and Loyola exclaimed together.

"The owner says it loves to run in wide-open spaces."

"Yes, but the *cemetery*?" Trevor repeated.

Trevor knew a bit about the old Twillingate Cemetery. He passed by its ugly iron gate every day on his way to and from school.

The signs posted next to the gate were bleak:

Beware of Falling Gravestones
Enter at Your Own Risk
Closed at Sunset
No Dogs Allowed

Inside, the cemetery was even more ominous. It was jammed with ancient gravestones toppling this way and that. There were some benches and a hedgerow, and beyond that there was the newer part of the cemetery with much plainer markers arranged in straighter lines. There were never any visitors, or dogs for that matter, which added to the forlorn look of the place.

"The cemetery's no place for lost dogs," he said to Ms. Wentzell. "Mr. Creelman would never allow it."

Mr. Creelman was the cemetery's elderly grounds-keeper. He was in charge of a small group of equally elderly men called the Twillingate Cemetery Brigade. They cared for the grounds and made repairs to the grave-stones in need of cleaning. When they took breaks from their work, they hung out at Sacred Grounds Cafe nearby, which was famous for its excellent lasagna. Trevor knew all this because Mr. Creelman had once been a guest speaker at the Queensview Mystery Book Club.

Trevor joined the Queensview Mystery Book Club as soon as it was formed, back at the beginning of grade six, because he had always loved solving riddles. The club was one of the reasons that Queensview was better than any other school he'd been to, which was four so far.

When Mr. Creelman visited the club, he talked about how to uncover buried family secrets by studying grave markers. He also told them about the history of the stone carvers at Twillingate Cemetery and what the symbols meant. Then he hauled out a book called *Famous Last Words* and grimly recited one gravestone poem after another in his gravelly monotone voice.

Trevor shook his head at the memory.

The school bell rang.

Ms. Wentzell returned to her desk but Trevor lingered, pretending to study the large map of the world on the wall near the window. He was waiting for Loyola to leave so that he could retrieve his book without her help. But she took forever to sign out her tall stack of books.

Trevor studied the map some more, trying to remember which countries his parents, both pilots, were flying to that week. His bedroom was filled with things from around the world that they had brought back from their trips — various globes, a plush monkey who bicycled across a tightrope strung between two walls, curious action figures that looked like astronauts, puzzle books, spinning tops, exotic model cars, dancing marionettes and musical instruments that made strange sounds.

Because Trevor's parents were working their way up to becoming captains by gaining experience flying different types of airplanes under different types of conditions, they had to jump at job openings when they had the chance. In fact, they were moving again for their next assignment right after Trevor graduated from grade six, which was in three months.

"Don't you both have your photo session now?" Ms. Wentzell asked.

All the club photographs for the yearbook were being taken that morning.

"I almost forgot!" Loyola exclaimed as she stacked her last book under her arm, then bolted.

Trevor immediately made a beeline for the rolling footstool, heaped some more books on it, climbed up, and, teetering like mad, snatched *The Case of the Way-laid Water Gun* from the loathsome top shelf.

By the time he finished signing his book out, the school's hallways were empty.

Trevor checked the wall clock. He could still make the photo shoot for the Queensview Mystery Book Club if he hurried. He dashed to the gym, knowing exactly what he would see. There would be a spot at the end of the front row saved for him. And, in the very middle of the back row, Loyola would be lording over everyone, surveying the tops of the heads before her. It would be just like their grade-six class picture taken at the beginning of the year all over again.

Trevor pushed through the gym door but stopped in his tracks. The gym was empty. Had he missed the photo session?

"Trevor!"

He turned at the sound of his name. It was Ms. Albright, the school's secretary, hustling down the hallway toward him.

"I thought I saw you rush by. I just told Loyola there's been a change of plans. The Queensview Mystery Book Club photo is being taken outside on the soccer field. If you hurry, you can still make it."

"Thanks," Trevor said, and he charged past her through the back door to the schoolyard, where it was unusually warm for April.

"Wait!" Trevor yelled as soon as he spotted his club on the field. The photographer had arranged the members sitting in a semi-circle, and they were reading mystery novels, including Loyola.

Mr. Easton, Trevor's grade-six teacher who was also new to the school and who had founded the club, stood and waved him over. The photographer stepped back from his tripod.

"Have a seat between Noah and Jennifer," Mr. Easton instructed as he returned to his own spot.

Trevor plopped down with relief — relief that they would be sitting for the photo and not arranged according to height like all the other school shots he had ever been in. He opened the book he had just signed out and turned to chapter one.

"Ready?" the photographer directed.

On cue, everyone turned to their books once again, except Miller, another member of the club, who was secretly giving Noah rabbit ears.

Click, click, click.

"All done," the photographer announced.

Mr. Easton stood to chat with the photographer as he packed up his equipment.

"Where were you?" Noah asked.

"At the library," Trevor said. "Why?"

"Mr. Easton posted the assignments for community service duty."

"Where?"

"On the wall just outside the classroom."

Trevor knew that all grade-six students had to volunteer for three months of community service in order to graduate from Queensview.

Noah stood up.

"What'd you get?" Trevor asked, standing, too.

"I'm helping out at the veterans' hospital."

"That's what I wanted!" Trevor said.

"Oh, that's too bad. It's full now."

"That's okay. Maybe I got the soup kitchen," Trevor said. It was his second choice.

"That's full, too," Jennifer said, eavesdropping. "I got that, along with Bertram."

"Really? Then what did I get?" Trevor asked.

"Don't know," Noah said. "Go find out."

Trevor didn't hesitate. He trucked past the playground

equipment where a few of the birdhouses his class had made from outdated textbooks were still hanging.

Mr. Easton was always getting them to do fun projects like that. Another time he had his students write poems about the sky on kites that they had made. Then they flew the kites in the schoolyard. Trevor had written about the vapor trail that airplanes leave behind. His parents got all weepy when he read that poem to them, and they had it framed.

Trevor pushed those memories aside as he re-entered the school. His classroom was upstairs, across from the music room. It felt like an eternity to reach it, but there on the wall, next to the door, was a large sheet of paper titled *Community Service Assignments*.

Trevor scanned the sheet as fast as he could. As he read the penned-in names of his classmates, his concern grew. Gone were his first, second and third choices. Then, at the very bottom, Mr. Easton had written Trevor's name in his left-handed, loopy, backward-slanted penmanship.

Trevor read the name of the organization to which he had been assigned.

The Twillingate Cemetery Brigade.

Trevor heard a gulp behind him.

He turned around and looked up.

Way up.

And then he spun back to the list on the wall just to be sure.

It was true.

Her name had been written right beside Trevor's in that same loopy, backward-slanted handwriting, filling the only other spot for the Twillingate Cemetery Brigade.

Loyola Louden.

Two

—

Pet Patrol

"You got the cemetery, too," Trevor stated, slowly turning around to face Loyola.

Loyola nodded, still staring over the top of his head at the sheet of paper in horror.

"Was that your first choice?" he asked.

Loyola shook her head.

"Second choice?"

Loyola shook her head.

"Then I'm guessing it wasn't your third, either."

Loyola's forlorn look said it all.

Trevor could see that it wasn't the cemetery that horrified her. It was the grim realization that she and Trevor would be paired *together* for this assignment.

She took a giant step back.

Trevor wasn't offended. He didn't like the idea, either.

"How does this work again?" he asked from the safer distance she had created.

He was a little vague on the details. After all, he had been attending Queensview Elementary for less than a year, and every school he had ever been to came with a different set of rules. The whole community service requirement was new to him.

"We have to volunteer for a charity for three months. Every Wednesday afternoon. From now until school ends in June."

Loyola rattled off the details in a mechanical, deadpan voice, as if she were in shock.

She took another giant step back, attempting to shrink into the row of lockers across from where Trevor stood.

"Together?" Trevor said. "You and me?"

"I don't think there's any other choice," Loyola said glumly, her back pressed against the lockers, nowhere else to go. "The rest of the list is completely full." Her voice softened to the point of almost disappearing.

But there she stood, larger than life. She turned to open her locker.

"Let's talk to Mr. Easton," Trevor said, taking charge, because she certainly didn't look as if she was up for the challenge. Then he gasped. "Whoa!"

She had swung the locker door open, and for the first time Trevor got to see the contents. Her clothes hung on hangers, her spare shoes were stacked in boxes on the floor with pictures of them taped to the fronts so that she could tell which pair was inside, and her books and notepads were neatly arranged on the top shelf according to height and color.

It was the most organized space he'd ever seen!

Loyola ignored his awe. She deposited her mystery novel on the top shelf, then shut the locker door.

Some of the other grade-six students had started drifting back into class from the photo shoot. Trevor and Loyola stayed put, craning their necks to look for Mr. Easton. They both spotted him at the same time as he made his way down the hallway toward their class, surrounded by more students who were joking with him.

"Mr. Easton," Trevor called out as soon as their teacher was within earshot. "Can we talk to you for a second?"

Mr. Easton slowed his pace.

"What's up?" he asked as the other students slid past him and took their seats inside the classroom.

"It's about community service duty," Trevor said. "I know that not everybody could get their first choice ..."

"But there must be room for us in another group," Loyola chimed in from her safety zone across the hall.

"I'm afraid there isn't," Mr. Easton said. "Besides, the Twillingate Cemetery Brigade really needs the school's help."

Trevor glanced at Loyola, who had begun to slouch in defeat.

Mr. Easton paused.

"Is it because of the cemetery? Surely you don't believe in ghosts," he said, misreading their stricken faces.

Trevor hadn't thought of that. Maybe he and Loyola could be reassigned if they claimed an irrational fear.

"Yes, that's it," Trevor declared, hoping Loyola would follow his lead and play along. "Grave markers give me the creeps."

Mr. Easton looked as if he didn't believe the ruse for a second.

"And all those gravestone poems about dead people?" Trevor grimaced.

"Epitaphs," Mr. Easton corrected.

"Epitaphs," Trevor repeated. "Pretty bleak, am I right?"

"Not as bleak as you might think. I read the description of the work that the Twillingate Cemetery Brigade undertakes. They'll be covering topics like how to read eroded inscriptions, how to clean a gravestone, how to map locations of the plots and how to take rubbings of epitaphs. There's even a lesson on how to design your own gravestone."

"Design my own gravestone?" Trevor repeated incredulously.

Mr. Easton's unwaveringly cheerful tone made it sound as though he was describing a fun-time theme park. It dawned on Trevor that he was not going to make any headway pretending to be afraid of cemeteries.

"I should think it would be fascinating," Mr. Easton continued. "Mr. Creelman has designed his own gravestone. He told me it features thistles from his parents' home country of Scotland, along with an epitaph inspired by the planetarium where he used to work."

Trevor looked over at Loyola, but she was still no help, having glumly planted herself on the opposite side of the hallway, secret pact in full force.

Was Mr. Easton aware of their secret pact? Had he ever noticed that they wouldn't be caught dead standing next to each other?

"Don't look so morose," Mr. Easton said kindly. "Twillingate Cemetery isn't a death sentence."

He started to chuckle at his pun. Trevor and Loyola did not join in.

Mr. Easton stopped chuckling. He sighed.

"Okay. Tell you what. I'll see what I can do. But no promises."

"Great!" Trevor said with relief, thinking that he could slide into one group on the list, Loyola could be sent off with another group, and their secret pact would be safe.

Problem solved.

"No promises, Trevor," Mr. Easton repeated, trying to sound stern, but Trevor knew better. "I haven't any idea what I'm going to say to the Twillingate Cemetery Brigade. They're going to be very disappointed."

Before Mr. Easton could change his mind, Trevor made a hasty retreat into the classroom and sat at his desk in the front row. Loyola did likewise, only her destination was a desk at the very back of the room where she surveyed everyone's comings and goings. She reminded him of a control tower looking down at all the puny airplanes on the tarmac. Between them, hanging from the ceiling above their heads, floated another of Mr. Easton's playful assignments, this time about setting words free. He had had his students fold the pages from a manuscript he had been working on into bats or birds or dragonflies, turning them into mobiles of fluttering words marked up with red ink.

There wasn't much class time left before the lunch bell rang. Trevor ate with some of the other boys in grade six. He had made friends quickly, but, as usual, he had only learned one or two key facts about each of them, knowing he'd be gone in a year.

"So what did you get for community service?" Miller asked while scarfing down his roast beef sandwich. Miller had broken his arm twice last summer.

"Cemetery duty," Trevor said, but hastened to add, "Mr. Easton is going to change it."

"Cemetery duty?" Miller repeated between bites. "With that old man who came to the Queensview Mystery Book Club?"

"Mr. Creelman? Yes," Trevor said. "But like I said, Mr. Easton's going to change it."

"Do you remember his eyebrows?" Craig said. Craig was constantly stuffed up with allergies and talked through his plugged nose.

Trevor remembered. Mr. Creelman's eyebrows were like puffy white cotton balls.

"Who wouldn't," Trevor said, digging into his cheese sandwich. He ate one every day without fail, one of the few constants in his life.

Miller wiped his hands on his pants, then, frowning, plucked a bag of fresh baby carrots from his lunch bag with two fingers, as if he was handling something that had gone moldy.

"And those poems," Bertram added. Bertram was the writer in the group, having recently recited a hilarious poem about his grandmother's yard sale that had had the class in stitches. "Mr. Creelman covered everything you'd ever want to know about death, and then some."

"I told you, Mr. Easton is going to find me something else to do for community service," Trevor insisted.

"Who else got assigned cemetery duty?" Miller asked, munching through the carrots faster than a garden of rabbits.

Trevor set down his sandwich. He was losing his appetite. Perhaps he needed to hang out with a different crowd at lunch. This bunch was merciless!

They all stopped chewing and stared at him for an answer.

"Loyola," Trevor finally muttered.

He braced himself.

The boys — every single one of them — whooped.

"That's classic!" Noah said. He liked to use big words. "You and Loyola? Stomping around that lumpy old necropolis together!"

Trevor was pretty sure that *necropolis* was a fancy word for graveyard.

"It's not going to happen," he insisted with a dismissive wave of his hand.

"What a spectacle," Noah went on with his lethal word choice. "And I'm not talking about the ghosts and other apparitions."

"The dynamic duo," Craig added, following Noah's lead. "Able to reach high shelves *and* fit into small spaces. That's quite the combination."

"Very funny," Trevor said.

He could see that it might actually be funny if it hadn't been about him. This kind of remark was exactly why he and Loyola had a secret pact not to stand next to each other.

"What's an apparition?" Miller asked Noah, having polished off his carrots.

"An apparition?" Noah repeated. "It means ghost-like."

Trevor seized the opportunity to steer the conversation away from Loyola.

"So you believe in ghosts?" he asked Noah.

"Why wouldn't I?"

"Have you seen any?" Trevor asked.

"No," Noah said. "I wouldn't be caught dead in that cemetery."

Miller jumped in. He had scooped out the contents of his first pudding cup and had already started to peel back the lid of the second one, which he had happily discovered deep in his lunch bag.

"Noah's right. There are definitely ghosts at Twillingate."

All the boys turned to Miller. He continued his spooky account between spoonfuls.

"People say there's one ghost in particular. It's a man who's searching for his wife. He wanders from gravestone to gravestone in the middle of the night, looking for her name."

"She's not buried beside him?" Bertram asked.

"No. That's the thing. When he died and was buried, his family placed a double marker on his grave. On his side of the marker is his name and dates and all that, but the other side is completely blank."

"Maybe his wife hasn't died yet," Bertram reasoned, but his eyes were wide open. He was clearly creeped out.

"Do the math. He's been dead for over two hundred years," Miller explained, his words hanging over them like ominous black clouds.

The boys grew silent, pondering the mystery, except for Trevor. He rolled his eyes.

"You think I'm making this up?" Miller demanded.

"I'm sure it's true. Every word," Trevor said, playing along.

"Well, get this," Miller said, pulling out a muffin from his bottomless lunch bag. "On the dead man's side of the grave marker, it reads that he was an affectionate husband. Only the word *affectionate* was scratched off and it had to be carved back in again even deeper than the other words surrounding it. They say that his wife's ghost erased her side of the grave marker and then scratched out *affectionate* when she was buried next to him. Apparently, he wasn't such an affectionate husband after all."

"Wow," Trevor said in a deadpan tone, continuing to goad Miller so as to keep everyone off the topic of Loyola. "That's quite a story."

"You still don't believe me?" Miller asked, and then he tackled his muffin in five quick bites.

Trevor decided not to press his luck. Unlike the others, he knew a thing or two about when to stop teasing. Instead, he gave a noncommittal shrug.

Having polished off the muffin, Miller reached over and plunged his hand into Bertram's open bag of chips.

"Hey!" Bertram complained.

"Go by and have a look," Miller taunted Trevor. "No, wait! You have cemetery duty, so you'll be able to check it out any time you want."

"There are no ghosts," Trevor insisted. "There are no vampires or werewolves, either. Besides, I told you. Mr. Easton's going to find me something else to do."

"Yeah, probably," Miller agreed.

Mr. Easton had certainly come to his rescue plenty of times throughout the year.

Miller began to root around his lunch bag for something else to eat, but came up empty at last.

"What about zombies?" Craig asked. "Do you have an opinion on those?"

"The undead who walk around confused and constantly hungry?" Trevor said. He nodded in Miller's direction. "Sure there are zombies. We have living proof."

The boys laughed as the school bell rang, announcing that lunch was over.

Trevor was relieved that their conversation had ended, but continued to worry about whether or not Mr. Easton could get him out of cemetery duty with Loyola.

Of course he could, Trevor reasoned to himself. Mr. Easton was probably the kindest teacher that he had ever met, and he had been to four schools so he had plenty of comparisons.

Up until grade six, Trevor had been too busy quickly learning the rules of each new school and making a few friends to care much about his teachers. Meeting Mr. Easton changed all that. He had gotten to know each of his students so that he could recommend a book they would be sure to like. It was his idea that Trevor might want to borrow *The Case of the Waylaid Water Gun* from the school library.

On his way back to class, Trevor ran into Mr. Easton, who was stooping in front of the water fountain in the hallway.

"Did you find something else for me to do for community service?" he asked, boldly pushing his luck.

"I did get a chance to call the Twillingate Cemetery Brigade over lunch, and I spoke to Mr. Creelman," Mr. Easton said, wiping his mouth with the back of his hand.

"You did?" Trevor said.

"He was very disappointed."

"Oh," Trevor said, feeling his chest collapse. What else could he say?

"He told me that the Twillingate Cemetery Brigade has been working with student volunteers for years."

Trevor's sinking feeling told him that he would not like where this conversation was headed.

"But I hear that cemetery really does have ghosts," Trevor blurted out. Even *he* didn't know where he was going with that malarkey. A bid for sympathy, maybe?

"Ghosts?" Mr. Easton repeated. "Seriously?"

Trevor nodded, hoping his absolute disbelief in the undead did not betray him. And then he remembered that Mr. Easton was also new to the school, having arrived for grade six just like Trevor. Perhaps he was unaware of the town's ghost story, too.

"They say there's this one who is missing his wife. He goes around looking for her name on the other grave markers."

"Is that so? And who told you this?"

"I don't know," Trevor said, studying the floor. "I just heard it."

Trevor knew that if he had said, "Miller," it would be game over. He and Mr. Easton, and everyone else for that matter, understood that Miller made up stuff all the time.

Embellishing, as Mr. Easton liked to call it.

Mr. Easton studied Trevor. Then he sighed.

"You can relax," Mr. Easton said, running his hand through his thick, wavy hair. "Mr. Creelman only wants volunteers who are committed to the work. He wants volunteers who love and appreciate the cemetery as much as the Twillingate Cemetery Brigade. The grounds are very important to them and to the families of those who are buried there."

"Mr. Creelman told you all that?" Trevor asked.

Was Mr. Creelman trying to make him feel guilty?

It was working. Trevor scuffed at the floor.

"He did," Mr. Easton said. "But he's letting you off the hook."

"What will I do now?" Trevor asked, not feeling nearly as much relief as he had hoped.

"Interestingly enough, Mr. Creelman had a suggestion that I followed up on."

"What?" Trevor asked warily.

"Mr. Creelman told me that the local animal shelter has started a new program called the Pet Patrol and they are looking for volunteers."

"The animal shelter? Isn't that where they take care of lost cats and dogs?"

"They do. And they've started a program for senior citizens who own dogs that need exercise and an opportunity to socialize with other dogs. Volunteers pick up the pets from their homes and take them for a walk. That way the dogs stay healthy and happy."

"So I would be a dog walker?" Trevor asked. He was quickly warming to the idea. In fact, he couldn't believe his luck. He loved dogs, but he didn't own one because his family moved so much.

"How does that sound?" Mr. Easton asked.

"You're the best!" Trevor exclaimed.

"Well, you really ought to thank Mr. Creelman."

"I will," Trevor said generously, knowing full well that he would likely never run into Mr. Creelman again with his family move so near at hand.

The next Wednesday afternoon, Trevor reported to the animal shelter. It was located five blocks from Queensview Elementary in the direction of the town's public park. As he pushed through the front door, a bell tinkled, announcing his arrival. Inside, it smelled of soap and warm dogs and lasagna.

"Hello," he said to the woman wearing a white lab coat sitting behind the front desk. She was eating lunch from a take-out box that had *Sacred Grounds Cafe* printed on its lid. "I'm Trevor. I'm here from Queens-view Elementary to volunteer."

"Oh, yes. The Senior Citizens' Pet Patrol. But I was told there'd be two of you."

"Two of us?" Trevor repeated. "Mr. Easton didn't tell me about another volunteer."

"Yes," the woman in the lab coat said. "It's the school's policy. Students must work in pairs for safety reasons."

The bell tinkled behind him. He turned.

And he looked up, way up, in disbelief.

It was the school giant, dressed to be invisible in a faded gray sweater and dark brown pants.

"What are you doing here?" Loyola demanded, for-getting to use her I'm-smaller-than-I-look voice.

"I got out of cemetery duty," Trevor announced loudly, so as to take up as much space as possible. "And you? Did you lose a dog? Or a cat?"

"Don't be ridiculous," Loyola said hotly, but keeping her distance. "I got out of cemetery duty, too."

"Well, we can't *both* be here," Trevor reasoned. "Go back to the school and find something else for com-munity service."

"You go back," Loyola argued. "I like dogs."

Loyola held her ground, arms crossed, but at a safe distance from Trevor. Trevor stood firm, too.

"There are plenty of dogs to go around," the woman in the lab coat cut in jovially, ignoring their standoff.

Obviously, she did not know about their secret pact.

"Here you are," she said, handing Trevor a plastic vest with a chest-sized reflective *X* on the front and back. It was the kind of vest that crossing guards or construction workers wore so that motorists could see them in blizzards or fog.

She handed a vest to Loyola, too.

"One size fits all," the woman in the lab coat added cheerfully.

Was she trying to be funny? Trevor wondered as he reluctantly put on his vest.

"Here are your walkie-talkies. They have a long range in case you need me."

She showed them how to work the buttons.

"And here's the list of addresses of the senior citizens to whom you've been assigned."

She retrieved the list from her desk and handed it to Loyola.

Trevor frowned. He knew Loyola got the list because she looked older than him. She looked older and more responsible just because of her height. It wasn't fair.

"We're the same age," he wanted to state for the record, but he didn't. He thought that it would make him sound small.

Loyola studied the list.

"Are all the addresses near here?" she asked, returning to her soft voice, her I'm-smaller-than-I-look voice.

The woman in the lab coat nodded as she pulled out a map from the drawer of her desk and laid it out for them. She pointed to their location.

"Here's where we are," she said. "And here's the park where you might want to take the dogs. The seniors live on these blocks between the two."

"They're very close by," Trevor observed out loud to show that he was perfectly capable of reading maps, despite being short.

"That's right," the woman said. "You'll have six dogs between you so be sure to keep them on their leashes. And remember to wear your vests and use crosswalks at all times."

"Will do," Trevor said, using his large I'm-responsible voice. He was still smarting over Loyola getting the list of addresses. He turned to leave.

"Oh! One more thing," the woman in the lab coat said.

She pushed through a swinging door behind her desk, and Trevor heard different barks start up, with every dog sounding desperate for companionship.

"You keep the dogs back there?" he asked when she returned seconds later, and all the barking stopped.

"Dogs, cats and one bunny at the moment," she said. "They're waiting for good homes."

"Someone called our school looking for a lost dog," Trevor said.

"Lost, abandoned, runaways. We take care of them all," she said.

She handed Trevor and Loyola a clump of plastic bags each.

"What are these for?" Trevor asked.

"Doo-doo," the woman said with a smile. "It's the town's by-law. Don't worry. The bags are biodegradable."

That was *not* what Trevor was worried about. He had never had to pick up dog poop before. Could he even do it?

"You better get going," the woman said, eyeing the clock on the wall. "The seniors are expecting you. When you have finished your walk and returned the dogs, please report back here before you go home for the day. Have fun!"

"Tell you what," Loyola said as soon as she was outside, a sour look on her face. "There's no need for *both* of us to go to each house on this list. That's not very efficient and the dogs won't get as long a walk. So why don't I take the addresses that are on one side of the street, and you take the addresses on the other?"

"Sounds like a plan," Trevor said, just as happy not to be seen with her as she obviously was not to be seen with him.

She pulled out a notepad from her knapsack and began to copy out half the list of addresses for Trevor in her teeny-tiny handwriting.

"What about the park?" he added.

Regardless of their secret pact, the park was big

and he did not want to get lost on his own with three strange dogs.

Loyola hesitated with her pen, weighing her options, which were as limited as his.

"Why don't we meet at the park gate by the water fountain once we've picked up all the dogs, then figure out what to do."

She handed Trevor his list of addresses.

"Okay, time to fly," Trevor said, using a favorite family expression.

With that, Loyola crossed the street taking giant strides and started up the opposite sidewalk to the first address on her list.

Trevor was left in the dust.

Get used to it, he thought glumly.

Three

———

Dogs

Trevor trailed Loyola by about a half a block from his side of the street. He came to his first address: *Mrs. Tanelli, 657 Willow Lane*. Trevor climbed the crumbling concrete front steps of the little blue house and rang the doorbell.

Barking erupted from behind the door, the type of bark a small dog makes when it means business despite its size.

"Down, Misty. Down, girl," chided an elderly voice from within. The barking quieted.

The door slowly creaked open. A tiny lady, her hair in a tight bun, stood with a puffy white poodle at her heels. The poodle was sitting at high alert, her black eyes trained on Trevor. She growled slightly, which did nothing to intimidate him, since he was certainly not afraid of poodles.

"My name's Trevor. I'm a volunteer from the animal shelter," he said. "I'm here to walk your dog."

"Wonderful!" Mrs. Tanelli said, clasping her hands together. "Come in, come in! Misty can't wait. Now, where did I put her leash?"

Trevor eased himself into the house. Misty did not look thrilled. Mrs. Tanelli wandered into the kitchen in search of the leash, leaving him in a face-off with the suspicious poodle.

"You're gutsy. I'll give you that," Trevor said to Misty.

"Would you like anything to drink?" Mrs. Tanelli called from the kitchen. "I can make tea."

"No, thank you. I better keep going. I have other dogs to pick up."

Mrs. Tanelli wandered back into the hallway, bright pink leash in hand.

"Here you are," she said, clipping it to Misty's collar. "Now, where's your coat?"

Misty cocked her head.

Mrs. Tanelli wandered into the kitchen again.

Trevor shifted from one foot to the other. A quick calculation told him that if each house took this long, he was never going to get to the park.

Mrs. Tanelli came back with a dog coat. No wonder Misty was on edge. The coat was black and white and patterned like a panda bear. It even came with a hoodie. The hoodie had two little black ears sewn on.

Trevor watched in amazement as Mrs. Tanelli draped the coat over Misty's back and zipped her in. Misty didn't even put up a fight.

"All set," Mrs. Tanelli said with pride as she handed the pink leash to Trevor.

Trevor made for the door with the panda in tow.

Once outside, he looked up his next address: *Mrs. Ruggles, 727 Willow Lane.*

Trevor walked along the sidewalk, Misty trotting beside him. She was surprisingly well behaved for a dog forced to wear a humiliating panda suit in public. He climbed the front steps to Mrs. Ruggles' house, a white bungalow with green shutters. He rang the doorbell, which sounded like the bells of a clock tower.

A couple of low barks signaled from deep inside the house, but then silence.

The door opened.

"Can I help you?" an elderly woman wearing gigantic, thick glasses asked.

"I'm Trevor. I'm here to walk your dog."

"Oh, that's right. I'm Mrs. Ruggles. And this ..." Mrs. Ruggles turned to look behind her, but came up empty. "Duncan! Come here, you rascal!"

From around the corner at the end of the hall waddled Duncan, an enormous tan-and-white bulldog. He plowed up to Trevor's feet, staring straight ahead, and didn't budge again.

Misty, whom Trevor had tied to the outside railing, began to whine.

"I see you've brought Misty," Mrs. Ruggles said, her brow furrowing. "You'll need to watch her around my Duncan. She's a bit of a hussy."

Trevor looked down at Duncan's tremendously wide and wrinkled head.

"Are you sure he wants to go for a walk?" he asked uncertainly. He had never seen a dog so disinterested, so impartial. His little curled-up tail stayed wedged to his behind.

"Sure he does!" Mrs. Ruggles exclaimed. She pulled a leash from a basket by the front door and attached it to his collar. The collar was navy with anchors printed all around it. "Off you go, Duncan. Walkies!"

"*Hurrumph*," Duncan said, nobody's fool, and shifted himself to face the door.

Misty whined louder.

"Okay. See you soon," Trevor said, and out the door he went with Duncan, who ignored Misty completely, despite her best efforts to distract him with her panda attire.

The last address on Trevor's list was *Mr. Fines, 869 Willow Lane.* It was a narrow two-story house with a large maple tree in the middle of the front yard. Trevor tied the two dogs to the railing and rang the bell.

Barking erupted, along with scratching behind the door. It was quite a frenzy.

"Poppy! Sit! Sit, Poppy, sit! Poppy! Sit! Sit, I say! Sit!"

Trevor turned to look at Misty and Duncan. Misty sat on high alert with her head cocked. Duncan stood stoically, staring into the middle distance at nothing at all, his gargantuan pink tongue hanging out to one side. He seemed oblivious to the hysteria inside the house.

Eventually, the door swung open.

"Hello?" a gray-haired man wearing a vest and a bow tie called out.

"I'm Trevor. I'm here to walk your dog."

"Jolly good. Do come in, Trevor," Mr. Fines said.

Mr. Fines had an English accent. Beside him, barely able to sit, was a medium-sized brown-and-white dog with soft jowls, droopy ears, wavy fur along her stomach and the backs of her legs, and a short, cropped tail. She was so wound up, she trembled with excitement. At least, that's what Trevor hoped she was trembling with. Her stubby tail did not stop wagging.

"This is Poppy," Mr. Fines said. "Poppy, this is Trevor."

Poppy shook her head and her ears helicoptered above her making flappity sounds. Some spit from her soft mouth hit the nearest wall.

Mr. Fines attached Poppy's leash and handed it to Trevor.

"Watch her around birds, I dare say," he warned. "She's an English springer spaniel."

When Trevor reached the sidewalk with all three dogs, he consulted his list. That was it. He now had to head to the park gate where he was to meet Loyola. He looked down the block and spotted her way up ahead, her assortment of dogs surrounding her.

Of course she was ahead, Trevor thought bitterly. It was those giraffe-length legs of hers. Not only would people surely point and tease as they walked together, but he also realized that he was going to have a hard time just keeping up with her. It would be utterly humiliating and far worse than her helping him reach the top shelf for a book.

Trevor looked down at his dogs, who seemed to sense that the park was nearby. All three pulled at their leashes, driving him toward Loyola, a head-on collision in the making.

Trevor looked around for the brakes.

There weren't any.

Loyola's dogs had gathered at the foot of the water fountain, drinking in great slurps, when Trevor arrived with his lot. He looked up at the fountain's five stone cherubs who were busy pouring water from seashells to the thirsty dogs below.

"You're here," Loyola said flatly and not at all welcoming. Her choice of clothing helped her blend into the gray fountain surrounded by trees with tall brown trunks.

Trevor wanted to tell her that he didn't like the idea of walking together any more than she did, but he decided that he was going to be big about their situation, even if she wasn't.

"Who do you have there?" he asked pleasantly as his own dogs started to drink from the fountain.

Loyola pointed to her first dog, a little white Scottie wearing a plaid neckerchief. His stumpy tail and triangle ears were pointed straight up. He looked like a hand purse.

"This is MacPherson. He attacks Frisbees."

"Why?"

"He was accidently hit by one when he was a puppy. Now he spends all his time on the lookout. If he gets hold of one, he'll chew it to bits."

Trevor petted MacPherson's small head. The dog barely acknowledged him and continued to scan the sky for any incoming missiles, now that he had had his drink.

"This is Ginger."

Loyola pointed to an Irish setter with glossy red fur, long ears, horsey legs and a whippy tail.

"She loves to run away and hide, or roll in things that smell."

"Great," Trevor said. "That's just what you want for a dog. A stinky escape artist."

"I thought so, too," Loyola said dryly. "And this is Scout. He's a former police dog, now retired."

Scout was a German shepherd. He was all business and studied Trevor as if Trevor was contemplating criminal activities, like vandalizing park signs with spray paint or stealing rare plants in the protected wooded areas. There were a few medals dangling from his collar, probably for bravery in the line of duty.

"Watch out," Scout seemed to say. "I'm on to you."

"Okay, well this is Misty, this is Duncan, and this is Poppy," Trevor said, pointing to each of his dogs. "Apparently, Misty has a thing for Duncan, Duncan couldn't care less, and Poppy is a menace to birds."

"Interesting pack," Loyola said.

"Agreed," Trevor said, and then, because there was no way out, he added, "Well, time to fly. Which path should we take?"

"You decide," Loyola said, looking away as if he wasn't even there.

Trevor had been to the park a couple of times during his year at Queensview Elementary. It was a large one for a small town, and a winding creek ran through the middle of it. There were foot bridges, a playground area for small kids and picnic grounds with a bandstand for families. There were many inside paths to take through the heavily wooded areas that led to some remnants of former stone fortifications. The wide outside path that circled the park was used by runners and bicyclists. Trevor thought that it would be the safest route. There would be less chance of a Frisbee encounter, fewer birds and not many places for runaway dogs to hide or roll in smelly things.

"Let's take the outside route," he suggested.

Loyola hesitated. Trevor could tell that she was working out some calculations in her head. Sure, there would be fewer Frisbees and birds, and there would be less chance of losing a dog or two. But the wide outside path that circled the park was also the one that was most crowded with people.

The more people, the more likelihood of teasing if they were seen walking together.

"Maybe I should go ahead," Loyola suggested.

"Why?" Trevor asked sharply. He knew exactly why, but he was taken aback by her overly belittling tone.

"You've got Duncan, and he's probably going to slow your group down."

As if on cue, the rest of the dogs stopped sniffing whatever they were sniffing and studied Duncan. Duncan, oblivious, seemed rooted to his spot and stared ahead at nothing.

Trevor, however, saw red. How dare she imply that just because Duncan had short legs he wouldn't be able to keep up with the rest of the dogs!

"What are you saying?" Trevor demanded, puffing out his chest and standing tall, as tall he could, anyway.

Loyola hesitated. She bent down to pet Ginger, already her favorite, no doubt because of Ginger's long prancing legs.

"I'm not saying anything," Loyola said quietly, stroking the dog.

Her face turned pink, which meant, of course, that she knew she was saying plenty.

Meanwhile, Poppy began to point like a bird dog, lifting one front leg and bending her knee, then staring transfixed at the upper part of a tree where two crows glared at them with their beady black eyes. Poppy started to tremble and whimper.

"Time to fly," Trevor repeated, seizing the opportunity to get moving. "And *I'll* take the lead because Poppy looks like she's going to explode."

He didn't wait for Loyola's agreement before setting off with Poppy, who kept looking back at the tree; Misty, who stayed glued to Duncan's side; and Duncan, who grunted as he toddled along the path at a modest but unshakeable pace.

Like a wide snow plow after a heavy winter storm.

Or a slow-moving conveyor belt crammed with over-stuffed holiday luggage.

"Good boy, Duncan," Trevor muttered from time to time, determined to keep ahead of Loyola's lot.

Duncan didn't acknowledge the encouragement. He just trudged along at his own unwavering amble, looking neither left nor right, and certainly not looking at Misty, who was practically dancing circles around him in her silly panda outfit.

Then, horror of horrors, Duncan steered to the side of the path and squatted down.

It was over pretty quickly, a fresh lump of poop on the ground. Duncan stood, scratched the ground with his back paws in a symbolic gesture to bury the evidence, then stared at the path ahead, patiently waiting for Trevor to pick it up.

"Right," Trevor said out loud, digging a plastic bag from his pocket and hoping his own bold voice would give him strength.

He braced himself, held his breath and started a countdown — three, two, one. He scooped the turd into the plastic bag, but even in his quickness he could feel its warmth through the plastic. He shuddered as he tossed the nasty package into a nearby garbage can as fast as he could.

He missed.

Shuddering, he had to pick it up, still warm, and toss it all over again.

For the entire duration of this ghastly procedure, Duncan did not appear to care one way or another. He just stood, staring in the direction of where they would go next, with Misty flouncing around him and Poppy lost in the treetops.

"Heel," Trevor said, and the three dogs fell into place.

They moved together like this for a while, until a trio of joggers rounded the bend. They slowed their pace, then stopped altogether when they came upon Trevor's dogs.

"Are these all yours?" one jogger asked while the other two petted the dogs.

"No, I'm a volunteer dog walker," Trevor explained.

"This one's adorable. What's his name?"

"Duncan."

"He's so handsome. Who is his girlfriend?"

"That's Misty. And this one's Poppy."

Poppy was once again scanning the treetops.

"Poppy's a birdwatcher," Trevor added, to explain the odd behavior.

"They're wonderful," said the second jogger between huffing and puffing.

Then all three burst into a fury of questions about the dogs. What did they like to eat? What were their favorite games? What were they bred to do?

Trevor didn't know any of the answers, but he loved the attention and so did the dogs — although it was hard to tell with Duncan. Trevor vowed to himself that he would go to the library later in the week to do some research about the dogs. That way he would impress the seniors whose dogs he was caring for and also be able to answer questions in the park.

But he wouldn't go to the school library. He'd go to the Loyola-free *public* library — the one with the stained-glass windows that stood across from the cemetery that he passed every day walking to and from school.

The joggers were getting ready to resume their run when Loyola caught up to them with her three dogs. The questions started all over again, but Loyola didn't know the answers to them, either, as she explained in her quiet voice. All the while, she kept glancing nervously at Trevor, and he kept glancing nervously at her, but no one paid them any attention. It was all about the dogs.

Trevor started to relax. He caught Loyola smiling once or twice, and she even laughed at one of their comments about MacPherson. It was strange, the two of them standing together with no one making an irritating comment about jockeys or basketball players.

Then, just as suddenly as the joggers descended upon them, they were off, leaving Loyola and Trevor standing alone with six dogs.

"That was nice," Trevor said.

"What was nice?" Loyola asked, right back to her usual standoffish self.

"Nothing," he said, not really surprised. For someone so big, she was awfully small-minded. "Time to fly."

Trevor took the lead again. He marched his dogs along, determined to leave Loyola well behind. Duncan grunted occasionally about the pace. Then Poppy and Misty each had a poop on the path, and Trevor had to repeat his ordeal with the plastic bags.

Minutes after dumping two more icky packages into a garbage can, Trevor was stopped in his tracks by another group of joggers. More questions. More dog petting. And when Loyola caught up, it was more of the same. Not one person commented on either of their heights. Once again, it was all about the dogs.

During the latter part of the walk, Loyola did not hang back as much. The distance between her group of dogs and Trevor's slowly narrowed, until, throwing all caution to the wind, they were practically walking together.

As they rounded the corner toward the fountain, back to where they had started, a solo walker came upon them. He also stopped to chat.

"What an impressive collection of dogs you own," he said.

"They're not ours," Trevor said. "They belong to some seniors in the neighborhood. We're volunteers who help exercise their dogs."

The walker patted each of the dogs while Trevor and Loyola introduced them by name.

There was something familiar about the walker. Trevor was sure that he had seen him before.

But where?

By the time the walker was petting the last dog, MacPherson, Trevor had figured it out.

"Hey, I know you," he said. "You came to our school."

"That's right," Loyola jumped in. "Mr. Easton invited you to speak about your book. You're a mystery writer."

"The Queensview Mystery Book Club," the walker said. "That was a few months ago."

"Edward Pond," Trevor said.

"Good memory!" Edward Pond said.

Trevor and Loyola introduced themselves.

"How's your manuscript coming along?" Trevor asked.

"Not good. That's why I'm here. My fictional villain pulled off his latest heist, and he's made a clean getaway aboard a ferry. But now I'm stuck on what to do with him in chapter six. I'm absolutely blocked, so I thought I'd take a walk and try to think like a detective about where he might go next."

"Scout is a retired police dog," Loyola said proudly, rubbing the head of the stoic German shepherd in her care.

The medals on his collar jingled.

"Is that right?" Edward Pond said. "I've never met one before."

Scout dismissed Edward Pond with a glance that said, "That's right, mister. I solved *real* crimes in my day."

Misty began to nudge Duncan playfully, and Poppy started pointing at the treetops with her bent knee.

"Well, don't let me keep you," Edward Pond said, taking their hints. He waved goodbye and headed down the path on his own.

"Good luck with chapter six," Trevor called after him, but Edward Pond was already lost in thought, thinking like a detective.

Trevor and Loyola gathered their dogs and walked over to the fountain. They let them grab a final drink before returning them to their owners. Duncan seemed particularly thirsty, as if he had walked the hardest, which maybe he had. Trevor watched him with a special appreciation.

"When I was little, I wanted to become a detective," Trevor said, making small talk while the dogs slurped away.

"You did?" Loyola said, turning to him.

She sounded genuinely interested. It was encouraging.

"I loved solving riddles and things."

"Me, too!" Loyola exclaimed. "Every Saturday my dad would wake me up with a new riddle, and I'd try to solve it over breakfast."

"Is that why you joined the Queensview Mystery Book Club?" Trevor asked.

"I guess so. That, and Mr. Easton. He's the best teacher I've ever had. He's also the one who got me to like writing."

"What do you like writing about?"

"The usual stuff," she said with a shrug.

"Like what?" Trevor said, pressing his luck.

"I like to take an idea and turn it upside down. Do you remember at the beginning of the year when we had to write about what we did on our summer vacation?"

Trevor nodded.

"Well, I decided to write about what I *didn't* do on my summer vacation."

"What didn't you do?"

"Anything fun, that's for sure."

"I spent the summer packing and moving here," Trevor said. "You had to have had more fun than that."

Loyola hesitated, as if thinking over her summer.

"No, it was pretty miserable. I was supposed to go to Camp Kitchywahoo with Jennifer, but Jennifer couldn't go on account of the stomach flu, so I got stuck in a cabin with a bunch of girls I didn't know."

"What's wrong with that? This is my fourth school. I'm always stuck with kids I don't know. All you need to do is learn one or two quick facts about each one, join the conversation, and there you have it. An instant circle of friends."

"It wasn't that easy," Loyola muttered.

"Why not?" Trevor asked.

"They were mean."

"Mean? How?"

Loyola shrugged and looked away.

"My height," she whispered.

That caught Trevor off guard. He never expected Loyola to say anything to him about her height. What was happening to their secret pact? Should he quickly change the subject to give her time to realize her mistake? He glanced at her.

She was studying her feet.

Her extra-large feet.

And Trevor, for the first time, felt sorry for her.

He was wrestling with what to say. Something kind, perhaps.

"We'd better get going," she said. "We still have to drop the dogs home before we return to the animal shelter."

The moment for kindness had passed. Trevor knew it, and he was sure that Loyola knew it, too.

But before they headed out of the park, a poster taped to the signboard near the park gate caught Trevor's attention.

"Look at that," he said, pointing to it.

The poster had the word *LOST* printed in bold letters above a photograph of a small spotted dog.

"I didn't see that when we came in. It must have just been posted."

"Do you think it's the same dog that we heard about at the library?" Loyola asked.

"Could be," Trevor said as he gathered up the dogs in his care.

One by one, they dropped off their dogs along each side of Willow Lane. Then Loyola, by far the faster walker when she wasn't forced to keep her distance behind Trevor, stood waiting for him at the door of the animal shelter so it would appear that they were a team.

Trevor nodded curtly to her, and then they entered the office without another word. The woman in the lab coat took their vests, walkie-talkies and unused plastic bags. She chatted with them about their adventure at the park, until their conversation was cut off by a telephone call.

"See you next Wednesday afternoon," she said, reaching for the telephone.

Once they stepped outside, Trevor and Loyola immediately went their separate ways. Trevor did not look back.

Trevor made good on his vow to learn more about his dogs. He visited the public library after school the next day. The public library was housed in a building that had once been a church, and as he climbed the granite steps, he noticed that there was scaffolding by one of the stained-glass windows.

Inside, the building still looked like a church with its high-arched ceiling, windows that shone like jewels and shiny marble floor. But all the pews were gone, and in their place stood tall stacks and stacks of library books.

After asking directions at the front desk, Trevor made his way down one aisle and located the collection about dog breeds. He groaned.

Top shelf.

Sighing deeply, he retrieved a nearby rolling stool and wedged it against a stack so it wouldn't move. He piled some books on it and climbed up to grab a large selection. Then he headed to the back of the library where there were research tables. Trevor sat down. He had the whole section to himself. At least he thought so.

"Hello, young man," said a gravelly voice.

Trevor twisted in his seat to see who was speaking to him.

His mouth went dry, as if he'd been caught red-handed.

It was Mr. Creelman.

Four

—

Lost

MR. CREELMAN was standing beneath the stained-glass window under repair, a plaque in his hand and a toolbox at his feet. Like the two elderly men with him, he was wearing bright orange coveralls with *Twillingate Cemetery Brigade* embroidered on the chest.

"Tell me when this is straight," Mr. Creelman ordered Trevor, one cotton-ball eyebrow raised.

He held the plaque to the wall underneath the windowsill and slid it up and down until Trevor called out, "It's straight."

One of Mr. Creelman's companions held the plaque in position, while Mr. Creelman slowly bent down to retrieve a drill from his toolbox. Then he drilled holes in the wall so that he could screw the plaque into place. When they were done, the second companion produced a broom and swept up the debris made from the holes.

Trevor tried to bury himself in his stack of books so as not to be further noticed.

Flying under the radar, as his parents put it — another family expression.

"You from a school around here?" Mr. Creelman asked as he locked his toolbox.

"Queensview Elementary," Trevor said automatically, and instantly regretted it. Why didn't he say he was homeschooled? He practically deserved what was coming next.

"Queensview? I was just there," Mr. Creelman said, knitting his brows together. "The Queensview Mystery Book Club. That's why I recognized you. You were sitting in the front row."

Here we go, thought Trevor. He's going to make a comment about my unusual height. Trevor braced himself.

"I spoke about stone carvers," Mr. Creelman explained to the two elderly men with him. "And then I read some epitaphs."

His two companions didn't say a word. They just nodded and stared at Trevor, as if he were under interrogation or something. It was unnerving.

"Queensview's a good school," Mr. Creelman continued. "They teach the kids about community service."

The two men nodded in agreement.

Trevor began to fidget. Any minute now, Mr. Creelman was sure to figure out that he was the one who didn't want cemetery duty and chose the animal shelter instead. The pile of books about dogs in front of him was a dead giveaway.

Trevor took a deep breath, stealthily reached across the table and turned the stack ever so slowly until the spines with the book titles faced away from Mr. Creelman.

"What are you reading?" Mr. Creelman demanded.

"Not much," Trevor said, feeling like an idiot as soon as he said it.

Mr. Creelman strode over to Trevor's table and picked up the book on top of the pile.

"*Today's English Bulldog: A Complete Guide,*" he read out loud. Then he pulled the stack of books around so that he could read the spines.

Mr. Creelman's eyes narrowed, his bushy eyebrows taking a dive to complete the frown.

"Do you own a dog?" he asked.

"No," Trevor said.

"Thinking of getting one?" Mr. Creelman asked.

"No," Trevor admitted. "We move too much."

"I see," Mr. Creelman growled.

Busted.

Trevor stared at his stack of books and felt very small. Very small, indeed.

Mr. Creelman picked up his toolbox and started to leave. The two elderly men fell into step behind him.

Mr. Creelman paused and turned back to face Trevor.

"Give my regards to Isabelle Myers."

"Who?" Trevor asked in a little voice.

"Isabelle Myers. The director of the animal shelter."

The woman in the lab coat, Trevor realized. He forced himself to swallow. He could feel his face burning bright red.

Without another word, Mr. Creelman and his two companions marched out of the library.

Trevor felt bad and he wasn't really sure why. Okay, so he had gotten out of cemetery duty because he didn't want to be paired with Loyola-the-giant. And even that didn't work out. But at least the dogs were fun, and they distracted people from making rude comments while he and Loyola were forced to violate their secret pact. The Twillingate Cemetery Brigade should surely understand that.

Having somewhat convinced himself that he had done nothing wrong whatsoever, Trevor tried to shake off his bad feelings by getting up and stretching his legs. Then he wandered over to the plaque that Mr. Creelman had installed beneath the stained-glass window.

"*Restored by the Twillingate Cemetery Brigade*," he read out loud.

He studied the window. It featured people wearing robes and sandals who were looking up at the sky, clasping their hands. Beams of light shone down upon them and then onto his stack of books.

The light was quite beautiful. Trevor felt bad all over again.

The next Wednesday afternoon when he reported for duty at the animal shelter, the same woman wearing a lab coat sat behind the front desk eating lasagna from Sacred Grounds Cafe. Loyola had not yet arrived.

"Are you Isabelle Myers?" he asked.

"Oh dear. Did I forget to introduce myself the last time you were here?" Isabelle Myers asked. "I spend so much time with animals, I sometimes forget my manners."

"That's okay," Trevor said. "Mr. Creelman said to say hi."

"Mr. Creelman? What a wonderful man! He does so much for the community. His work at Twillingate Cemetery is outstanding. I'm so glad he thought to suggest the animal shelter for Queensview Elementary's list of community service organizations."

"Me, too," Trevor said as the bell rang on the front door of the animal shelter.

It was Loyola in dark, dark greens. Having immediately spotted Trevor, she kept her distance, just as she had done the entire past week whenever they were about to cross paths in the school hallways or classroom. The secret pact was back on.

"Hey, isn't that the same poster we found in the park?" Loyola asked, pointing to the bulletin board near the door.

Trevor nodded. It was the one about the lost spotted dog.

"The owner keeps calling," Isabelle Myers said. "He's a senior citizen and he's in a desperate way. I don't suppose you could drop by his house on the way to the park? Assure him that you're a volunteer with the animal shelter and that you'll keep a lookout?"

"We can do that," Trevor and Loyola said together.

Isabelle Myers wrote the address on a piece of paper, which Trevor plucked from her as soon as she was done.

"Mr. Fester, 951 Willow Lane," he read out loud. "That's close to the park gate," he said confidently.

He took charge by tucking the paper into his pocket. She handed them their safety vests, walkie-talkies and plastic bags.

When Trevor and Loyola stepped outside, Loyola turned, towering over him, and demanded, "Do you want to go to Mr. Fester's house, or should I?"

This irritated Trevor no end, because *he* was the one with the address. He was about to point that out, but instantly knew that it wasn't a good enough reason for getting his way. Perhaps he could challenge her to a race, but then he remembered that he would have Duncan, and Duncan couldn't be rushed. Out of options, and resenting how Loyola was still towering over him, Trevor offered the only thing left.

"Tell you what," he said. "We'll pick up our dogs, just like last time, and meet at his house."

"Fine," Loyola said, sounding put out, and she strode off to pick up her first dog.

Trevor collected Misty, Duncan and Poppy in that order and headed to the new address. Loyola was waiting for him with her dogs on the front lawn of a little brick house with black shutters and a winding stone path to the front steps.

They tied up their dogs, then jockeyed on the porch for the best position. Trevor won that struggle by ducking in front of Loyola to be closest to the door.

He was so happy that he had managed to beat her, he was caught off guard when Loyola reached around him with her made-for-basketball arm to ring the doorbell.

"I've got it," Trevor insisted, a beat too late.

She pressed the bell with ease, then dropped her hand to her side.

Nothing happened.

"Strange," Trevor said.

"Do we have the right address?" Loyola asked.

Trevor pulled out the slip of paper and double-checked the address against the number on the house.

"Yes," he confirmed.

This time he knocked on the door with force.

Still not a sound.

Then they heard a shuffling noise inside the house, and the door slowly creaked open.

"Mr. Fester?" Trevor said at his first glimpse of the

elderly man inside. "We're volunteers with the animal shelter and we're here about your dog."

Mr. Fester stepped out from behind the door. He wore a shirt and tie, leather slippers and a woman's apron with big bold flowers.

"My dog!" he said hoarsely. "You found my dog?"

"No," Trevor said quickly, realizing his mistake. "Not yet, but we wanted you to know that we're going to keep a lookout."

Mr. Fester studied Trevor, then Loyola, then Trevor again. His eyes filled with tears. Trevor had never seen an old man cry before, not even his dad. It was horrible.

"Buster's been lost for days," Mr. Fester said, wiping his eyes with the back of his shaky hand. "Please, please find him."

"We're so sorry," Loyola said gently. "Where did you lose him?"

"At the park," Mr. Fester said. "One minute I took him over to the water fountain for a drink." He gulped. "The next minute I turned around but couldn't clap my eyes on him. He was gone."

Mr. Fester wiped his eyes again.

"We've seen your posters. Buster is white with brown spots. Can you tell us anything else about him?" Trevor asked.

"He's not a big dog, but not small, either. He's very smart and full of beans. He loves to hide my slippers. He sleeps on his back. He has the softest ears. And ..."

Mr. Fester's voice went all choky. Trevor couldn't stand much more.

"We're going to the park with these other dogs," Trevor said. "We'll look for Buster while we're there. We'll find him. Don't worry."

Mr. Fester nodded pitifully and shut the door.

"How sad," Loyola said. "Do you think we'll really find his dog? It's a big park."

"We can try," Trevor said, anxious to do something.

They untied their dogs and walked toward the park gate. The dogs drank from the fountain while they worked out a plan.

"I think we should go through the middle of the park by taking one of the paths that leads through the wooded area. That's probably where Buster is lost," Loyola suggested.

"There're too many paths through the wooded area. Finding the right one would be like finding an empty airplane seat on Thanksgiving weekend," Trevor said.

"What an odd comparison," Loyola said.

"My parents are pilots," Trevor said with a shrug. And then he continued. "I think our best bet would be to stick to the outside path that circles the park. That's where most people walk and we can ask them if they've seen a spotted dog."

Loyola mulled this over while Trevor waited for her to acknowledge his brilliance.

"I guess," was all she offered.

It was not the full-hearted endorsement he was looking for.

They gathered their dogs and began the walk. It wasn't long before they were stopped by a group of joggers.

The joggers asked the usual questions about the dogs, only this time Trevor was able to answer more of them. He was especially good at answering questions about bulldogs.

Then, when the joggers were about to move on, Trevor said, "We're looking for a spotted dog named Buster. Have you seen him?"

"You've lost one of your dogs?" a jogger asked, eyebrows raised in alarm.

"No, not us. The owner did. He wants us to keep a lookout."

"I haven't seen a spotted dog," the jogger said while his fellow joggers shook their heads in agreement. "But we'll let you know if we do."

The joggers headed down the path.

"You seem to know a lot more about dogs than last week," Loyola said.

"I went to the public library," Trevor said. "The one that used to be a church."

"I love that one!" Loyola exclaimed. "Especially the windows. I'm going to be a librarian someday."

Trevor wanted to say, "You'd make a great librarian because you can already reach the top shelves without a rolling stool," but he knew better. Still, he wanted to continue their conversation.

"I ran into Mr. Creelman at the library," Trevor said.

"You did?" Loyola said, eyes widening.

"He does volunteer work there, too," Trevor said.

"Did you talk to him?" Loyola asked in awe.

For some reason, Trevor wanted to sound brave, braver than he was, anyway.

"Sure, I did."

Duncan interrupted their conversation by pooping on the path.

Trevor cleaned it up with a plastic bag. This time he didn't shudder. Was it because Loyola was watching or because he was getting used to the icky task?

Before they could finish their conversation, another crowd of runners stopped by. Same questions about the dogs. And no one had seen Buster. Trevor and Loyola continued on their walk all the way around the park, with many stops along the way.

Sadly, no Buster.

"What are we going to tell Mr. Fester?" Loyola asked as the dogs had their final drink at the water fountain before going home.

"All we can report is that Buster's not at the park. But he's got to be somewhere. It's a small town. We'll find him."

When they arrived at Mr. Fester's house, neither of them wanted to knock or ring the doorbell. They both stood awkwardly on the porch, until Scout barked at Ginger, who was biting at the part of her leash tied to the railing in an obvious attempt to escape. Loyola was retying Ginger's knot when Mr. Fester opened the door.

"Buster?" he called out gleefully.

"No," Trevor said. "That was Scout. We went all around the park, but Buster wasn't there."

Mr. Fester's face fell. He was no longer wearing an apron. Instead, he was hugging a leather-bound photo album to his chest.

"My poor dog," he said sadly.

Trevor felt a lump in his own throat. He was convinced that there was nothing worse than a sad old man who had lost his dog.

"Don't worry. We'll keep a lookout for Buster this week. As soon as we find him, we'll let you know," Trevor assured him.

"Then I'll give you my telephone number," Mr. Fester said. "Come inside."

Loyola and Trevor stepped indoors, leaving the dogs tied to the railing and Scout guarding the whole pack, especially Ginger who was now tied with triple knots.

Mr. Fester disappeared into the kitchen. Between them and the kitchen were stacks and stacks of books crowding the hallway and all the way up one side of the stairs to the second floor. Mr. Fester returned and handed each of them a business card.

"*A Likely Story Used Bookstore*," Trevor read out loud. "Are you the owner?"

"I used to be," Mr. Fester said. "Years ago. The cards are still good though, because my telephone number is the same."

"*A Likely Story*. Is that the one on Tulip Street?" Loyola asked.

"Yes. It's right beside the florist, near the cemetery."

"Twillingate Cemetery," Trevor added, just for clarity.

"That's right," Mr. Fester said. "Buster likes to run there, too."

Trevor thought back to the sign posted at the cemetery gate. *No Dogs Allowed.*

"We'll keep a lookout," he assured Mr. Fester all the same.

When they were returning their gear to the animal shelter at the end of their walk, Trevor and Loyola reported on their sad conversation with Mr. Fester.

"Well, if you don't spot Buster, there's a good chance someone else will bring him here," Isabelle Myers reassured them. "If that happens, we'll take Buster home, don't you worry."

Still, Trevor worried. The memory of Mr. Fester's stricken face kept urging him to keep a lookout after school and to take different routes home. That way he would pass the tennis courts, the melted outdoor skating rink and even the preschoolers' playground with the squeaky swings. He walked by every place he could think of where a dog might like to run.

No Buster.

When he reported to the animal shelter the following Wednesday, Loyola was already there wearing her usual blend-in attire. She turned to him as soon as he came through the door.

"No sign of Buster," she reported sadly. "Not even here."

"I've been chatting with Mr. Fester on the phone all week," Isabelle Myers said. "Poor man. Perhaps you can swing by his house and reassure him."

Trevor and Loyola nodded.

Once outside, Loyola said, "Let's pick up our dogs and meet at Mr. Fester's house. We'll talk to him together."

Trevor easily agreed. He did not want to face Mr. Fester alone. It was just too sad.

He started down his side of the street and knocked on the door of his first house.

As soon as he did, barking erupted. It was Misty, fooling no one.

"Hello, Mrs. Tanelli. How's Misty today?"

"She's been a very good dog. We went to the beauty parlor this week, didn't we, Misty?"

Misty wore a pink bow in the poufy mound of snow-white fur on the top of her head.

"Now, where did I put your coat?"

Mrs. Tanelli wandered off to the kitchen. Misty sat down at Trevor's feet and looked up at him with a grin. Despite her ridiculous frilly accessory, Trevor smiled back and gave her a neck rubby. She smelled like lilacs.

"Here you go," Mrs. Tanelli said. Only this time it wasn't the panda jacket. This one featured a leopard print.

Misty stood patiently as Mrs. Tanelli zipped her in, then handed Trevor the pink leash.

"All set?" Trevor asked Misty.

She wagged her tail, which ended in a silly pom-pom. They set out for the next house.

"Hello, Mrs. Ruggles," Trevor said when she answered the door.

Duncan was nowhere to be seen.

"Duncan!" Mrs. Ruggles called out gaily from behind her gigantic, thick glasses. "Walkies!"

After what seemed like forever, Duncan appeared from around the corner. He trundled up to Trevor and stood stoically at the door, waiting for his leash like a condemned prisoner.

Was he happy? Was he grumpy? Impossible to tell.

Trevor patted his wide, wrinkled head all the same. Duncan grunted.

Outside, Misty whined, eager for Duncan's company.

Mrs. Ruggles squeezed past Trevor and looked out

the door at Misty. She adjusted her glasses, then clucked her tongue.

"Just look at that outfit. Hardly daytime attire," she muttered. "And that's no way to get my Duncan's attention."

Trevor looked down at Duncan, who was paying attention to no one at all.

Mrs. Ruggles clipped Duncan's leash to his collar with the anchor print.

"Good boy," she said.

If Duncan took her praise to heart, he certainly didn't show it. Instead, he grunted and shifted his massive bulk to face the door.

"All set?" Trevor asked.

Nothing from Duncan.

"All right, then," Trevor said, taking that as a yes, and they headed out.

Trevor tied both dogs to the railing of the third house. He rang the bell.

An explosion of barking erupted from somewhere deep inside the house and grew louder and louder until Trevor heard scratching and barking from right behind the door.

"Sit, Poppy! Sit! Sit! Sit, I say! Poppy! Poppy, sit!"

He looked back at his two dogs. Misty was prancing around Duncan. Duncan, unmoved, was staring at the back of his calves.

The door creaked open.

"Hello, Mr. Fines," Trevor said.

"Do come in," Mr. Fines said in his English accent while adjusting his bow tie.

Trevor stepped inside, and Poppy immediately jumped up on him, her mouth a wide smile, her stubby tail wagging a million miles an hour.

"Down, Poppy, down," Mr. Fines ordered. "Mind your manners!"

Poppy reluctantly dropped to all fours, but her shiny brown eyes were pinned on Trevor. She shook her head in glee, long ears flapping above her like a helicopter, spittle flying everywhere. One ear landed inside out. Poppy didn't seem to mind. Trevor flipped it back to rights all the same.

Outside, Misty yipped and pranced by the porch. Poppy heard the sound and pushed past Trevor to look out the screen door. Her tail started wagging all over again. It was a blur.

"How many dogs do you walk?" Mr. Fines asked.

"Three, including Poppy," Trevor said. "And my classmate, Loyola, also walks three. So we have six altogether."

"Six dogs? However do you manage?"

"We do all right," Trevor said proudly. And then, just to show off how responsible they were, he added, "We're also on the lookout for a lost dog."

"You lost a dog?" Mr. Fines said, worry creeping into his voice.

"No, not us. The owner did. He reported it to the animal shelter."

"Oh, how dreadful," Mr. Fines said. "I can't imagine life without Poppy."

"We'll find the dog," Trevor assured him.

"How will you know you've found the right one?" Mr. Fines asked.

"We have a good description. It has brown spots all over," Trevor said.

"I once knew a dog with spots," Mr. Fines recalled.

"I guess there must be lots of dogs with spots," Trevor said. He started to grow alarmed at his own realization. Finding Buster might be harder than he thought.

"Perhaps," Mr. Fines said. "But the spotted dog I once knew was quite unique. Very excitable even though it was old. It spent its days at my favorite bookstore keeping the owner company. The owner would read to that dog for hours at a time. If I recall correctly, the spotted dog loved movie scripts the best."

"That's funny," Trevor said. "The owner of the missing dog used to run a bookstore."

Mr. Fines, who had been stroking Poppy's ears, looked up.

"Are you talking about Heimlich Fester?"

"Yes, that's him," Trevor said with surprise.

"Oh dear," Mr. Fines said.

"What?" Trevor said.

"Heimlich sold his bookstore years ago."

"That's right. He told us that. It was called A Likely Story Used Bookstore."

Mr. Fines returned his attention to Poppy. He kept talking, but he no longer looked Trevor in the eye.

"Heimlich must be confused."

"Confused? What do you mean?"

"There's no need to keep a lookout for his dog."

"I don't understand," Trevor said.

"Heimlich's dog was fifteen years old when he sold his bookstore. And that was years ago. His dog couldn't possibly be alive today."

"Dogs don't live that long?" Trevor asked.

"I'm afraid not."

"Are you sure?" Trevor said.

Mr. Fines said nothing.

"Do you remember its name?" Trevor persisted.

"Buster," Mr. Fines said, handing Poppy's leash to Trevor. "The spotted dog's name was Buster."

Five

———

Tattle

"Time to fly," Trevor urged his dogs as soon as he was out of earshot of Mr. Fines, who waved them goodbye from his front porch.

Trevor was determined to catch up to Loyola before she reached Mr. Fester's house.

How sad that Mr. Fester was confused. And now they were going to have to tell him that there was no Buster after all. That meant the old man would be confused *and* sad. Trevor couldn't think of anything worse.

He spied Loyola up ahead almost as soon as he left Mr. Fines' house. She had gathered her three dogs and stopped to clean up after one of them. She dropped her unpleasant package in a nearby garbage can next to a mailbox.

"Loyola!" Trevor called. "Wait up!"

"Ginger's been a bad dog this week," Loyola reported as soon as Trevor joined her. "She broke out of her backyard and ended up being captured by the neighbors. Apparently, she was digging up someone's prize rose garden."

Trevor looked at Ginger, who smiled back and didn't look at all traumatized about her foiled escape. If anything, it looked as if she was planning her next runaway adventure.

"So I'm thinking," Loyola continued, "that if an escape artist like Ginger can be caught, then there's a good chance someone *will* find Buster."

"No, they won't," Trevor said bluntly.

"Why not?" Loyola asked.

"There is no Buster."

Loyola stopped in her tracks. "What do you mean?"

"I just learned that Buster has been dead for a long time. Mr. Fester is confused and thinks his dog is still around."

"Are you sure?"

"Mr. Fester sold his used bookstore years ago, and Poppy's owner just told me that Buster was an old dog, even back then."

"How awful," Loyola said. "So what do we do now? Do we tell him?"

"I don't think I'd be very good at that," he admitted.

"Me, either," Loyola said as if confiding to a friend.

She looked as if she might cry. Trevor almost felt like giving her a hug.

"Tell you what. Let's talk to Mr. Fester together," Trevor suggested.

"And what should we say?" Loyola asked, grateful for his company for once.

"We can remind him about how long ago he sold his bookstore. That might trigger his memory about Buster, and then he can piece it together himself."

"It's still sad," Loyola said.

Trevor nodded. He surveyed the six dogs. They were all looking in the direction of the park and fidgeting with excitement. Except Duncan. Duncan just stood, unfazed by the growing franticness surrounding him, perfectly content not to move for the rest of the day.

"Okay. Let's get this over with," Loyola said at last.

Together, they headed to Mr. Fester's front porch, Duncan grunting along. Trevor and Loyola tied the dogs to the railing. Trevor looked at Loyola. She nodded. He rang the bell. After what felt like an eternity, Mr. Fester answered the door.

Trevor glanced inside. The piles of books were still stacked everywhere in the main entrance and on up the stairs.

"Hello, Mr. Fester," Trevor said in a voice higher than normal.

"Oh, hello," Mr. Fester replied, hope creeping into his voice. "Are you here about Buster?"

"We're here to learn *more* about Buster," Trevor said, trying to trigger Mr. Fester's memories like they had planned. "Did Buster go with you to the bookstore when you owned it?"

"Yes, he did. I read to him every day. He was very good company. The customers loved him."

"Would you describe Buster as a calm dog?"

"Calm? Goodness no. He's full of beans."

"Is that why you used to read to him? To calm him down?"

"Yes."

Trevor was steering the conversation exactly where it needed to go.

"What type of books did he like best?"

"Movie scripts. That's why I named him Buster. It's short for Blockbuster. Blockbuster movies."

"That's a great name. When did you sell your used bookstore?"

"Nine years ago. The year after my wife passed away."

That caught Trevor off guard. It was sad to hear that Mr. Fester's wife had died. It was also unsettling that he seemed to remember everything very well. He didn't appear to be confused at all. So why was he getting them to chase after Buster?

"Oh," Trevor said. "I'm sorry about your wife."

He paused for a respectable moment before continuing.

"So then, you live by yourself?"

"No," Mr. Fester said crankily. "I have my books and I have Buster."

Trevor looked at Loyola, who looked as baffled as he felt.

"You certainly have a lot of books," Loyola interjected. "I'm going to be a librarian when I grow up. I love to shelve and categorize things."

"You should see her locker!" Trevor said, attempting to lighten the mood and keep the conversation going.

"That's admirable," Mr. Fester said. He paused and turned around to face the stacks of books behind him. "When I sold the bookstore, I took home quite a bit of the stock. I ran out of shelf space long ago, but I'm glad that didn't stop me."

"Because books are good company?" Trevor guessed. He had heard Mr. Easton say that to the Queensview Mystery Book Club on plenty of occasions.

"There's that, but also my late wife insists on playing cards with me."

Okay, so he *is* confused, thought Trevor. Dead wives can't play cards. And dead dogs can't be lost.

"You look alarmed," Mr. Fester said. "I've seen that look on my son. Don't be."

Mr. Fester fished something out of his shirt pocket. It was a playing card. The queen of spades. Only someone had drawn glasses on her face in red ink.

"See that?" Mr. Fester said, holding the card up for Trevor and Loyola to inspect.

"Queen of spades," Trevor confirmed.

"That's right. My wife was quite a card player. Bridge, mostly."

Trevor knew a little about bridge. He knew it was a complicated four-person game with many rules and many strategies. Partners played against partners, often in tournaments.

"You two liked to play bridge?"

"No, I wasn't a good partner. I'd rather be reading. But she and Arno Creelman won many championships."

"Arno Creelman? Do you mean Mr. Creelman? The one who takes care of Twillingate Cemetery?" Trevor asked.

"That's him," Mr. Fester said. "I still see him from time to time. Mostly at the grocery store. He was pretty mad when I sold the bookstore. He has quite a collection of his own books, especially about outer space and the solar system and such. He used to work at a planetarium."

"He came to our school," Loyola said. "To the Queensview Mystery Book Club. He read from a book of epitaphs called *Famous Last Words*."

"From his cemetery-care collection," Mr. Fester deduced. "Well, that's understandable. He lost his grandson to a car accident last summer. Terribly tragic."

Once again, Trevor was caught off guard, because once again, Mr. Fester seemed to be very clear on his facts, even tragic ones. No confusion there.

"I don't understand about the queen of spades," Trevor said.

Mr. Fester gently kissed his card before tucking it back into his left shirt pocket, the one over his heart.

"With all that bridge, I gave my wife a nickname. I called her the Queen. The Queen of Bridge. Before she died, she planted playing cards with queens all over the bookstore. Every once in a while, a customer would find one tucked into a random book. When you're in the second-hand book business, you find all kinds of things in books that people have used for markers. But I knew the playing cards were hers. She drew glasses on them. Red glasses. She had a pair herself."

"Oh. So that's how she's playing cards with you," Loyola said.

Mr. Fester nodded.

Trevor was baffled. He couldn't figure out Mr. Fester. Was he confused or not? Maybe there really was a Buster. Maybe Buster was just an incredibly old dog. Maybe Mr. Fines had it wrong.

"Well, time to fly," Trevor said, anxious to talk over the case with Loyola. "The dogs need their walk, but we'll keep a lookout for Buster."

"Please do," Mr. Fester said. "I miss Buster terribly. He was a stray when I found him. I know he can take care of himself, but still. I need to know that he's safe and happy."

Trevor and Loyola backed out the door and onto the porch. As they untied the dogs, Loyola spoke under her breath.

"What do you think?"

"Who knows."

All the way around the park and back to the animal shelter, they speculated as to whether Buster was real or a memory. But by the end of their walk, they had seen no sign of Buster.

Not one.

With Trevor's family move getting closer, talk around the dinner table was about all the good things to look forward to at the new place. Yet Trevor was often distracted. He remained troubled throughout the week. There was something about Mr. Fester's story. There was something not quite right. Trevor couldn't put his finger on it. So he continued to take different routes home, still looking for Buster and picturing Mr. Fester's sad face.

When he arrived at the animal shelter the following Wednesday, he and Loyola decided to stop by Mr. Fester's house with their dogs to see how he was doing. Mr. Fester opened the door and surprised them with a stack of posters.

"I made bigger ones," he said, after barely a hello.

He held up a poster for them to see. The words *REALLY LOST* were featured in big bold letters at the top. A new full-color picture of Buster lying beneath a park bench took up most of the poster. That was followed by details of who to call.

"Can you put these up for me?" Mr. Fester asked.

"Sure," Trevor said, feeling lost himself.

He and Loyola divided the stack in two and shoved them into their knapsacks.

That week Trevor put up all of his posters but wondered the whole time why he was even bothering. He chose lampposts around Mr. Fester's old bookstore, the children's playground and the melted outdoor skating rink.

And then it was May.

When the first Wednesday of that month rolled around, and Trevor and Loyola dropped by Mr. Fester's house, there was still no sign of Buster. There hadn't even been a single sighting. They weren't surprised. In fact, they were pretty sure there was no Buster. But it had become a habit to say hi and to chat with Mr. Fester, if only to keep him company for a little while. Even the dogs in their care knew the routine. All six of them would steer Trevor and Loyola to Mr. Fester's porch for a final stop before heading to the park for their Big Walk.

This time Mr. Fester handed them a box of dog treats.

"Put a few cookies under the benches around the park," he said. "Buster loves sitting beneath them. He might be getting tired of foraging for food, and I don't want him to go hungry."

Trevor took the box of dog treats and did as he was told.

"I don't know, Trevor," Loyola said, as he deposited the cookies underneath the first bench they came to. "This seems hopeless to me."

"It *is* hopeless," Trevor said, trying not to dwell on what he was doing. "And we're running out of time."

"What do you mean?" she stopped to ask.

"I'm moving at the end of the school year," he explained.

"Are you going back to your hometown?" she asked.

"Hometown?" Trevor repeated. "I've moved so often, I can't say I have a hometown."

"What's that like, moving so much?" Loyola asked.

"I'm used to it. I've gotten good at making friends no matter where I am."

"But then you have to leave them behind."

"I don't think about that as much," Trevor admitted with a shrug. "I think about the new ones I haven't met yet."

An awkward silence followed, so Trevor said what he always said to lighten the mood.

"Time to fly."

"You say that a lot," Loyola said.

The truth was, leaving classmates behind hadn't

bothered him very much because he had never had time to get to know anyone all that well. It meant that goodbyes weren't nearly as hard. And he had concluded a long time ago that it was better this way.

But what if it wasn't really better at all? What if he had gotten things wrong? That was not a happy thought.

It must have showed, because Loyola said, as if to cheer him up, "I think you're very brave."

Her praise worked. Trevor sat down on the bench and Loyola sat beside him. Then he gave a cookie to each of their six dogs, with an extra cookie for Duncan.

They went on to talk about other things during their walk around the park — their speculations about starting junior high in the fall, the strange ideas their parents had, their favorite foods, their favorite books, their favorite games to play.

Loyola even told him a hilarious story about her jokester great-grandmother who broke her hip and recovered in a hospital run by nuns. She went up and down the hallways with her walker wearing a hairband with red devil ears.

And Trevor told her the incredible story about how his parents unknowingly bought the exact same print by a local artist for each other to celebrate their recent anniversary. Both prints now hung side by side in their bedroom next to his framed poem about airplane vapor trails.

The only thing they didn't talk about was their different heights. That topic was still taboo, and they both knew it without having to say a word.

"So what do you really think is going on with Mr. Fester?" Loyola asked as they stopped at the water fountain so that the dogs could take a final drink before heading back.

"I don't think there is a Buster," Trevor admitted. And then he added, "I'm worried about Mr. Fester."

"Me, too," Loyola said. "It's awful that he's living alone."

Trevor remembered that Mr. Fester had mentioned a son who was worried about him. It would be a grown-up son, given Mr. Fester's age.

"Maybe his son could take care of him," Trevor suggested, recalling how his own parents phoned his grandparents on a weekly basis to make sure they were doing okay.

"Maybe. Let's see what we can find out the next time we drop by," Loyola said.

All that week, Trevor walked from school to home and back taking his regular straightforward route. By the end of the week, he realized that he had stopped looking for Buster without even knowing it.

"Hello, Mr. Fester," Trevor said the following Wednesday when Mr. Fester answered the door.

"Have you seen Buster?" Mr. Fester asked immediately.

It had become their sad routine.

"No," Trevor said, bracing himself for Mr. Fester's look of despair, which was sure to come.

It did.

"Oh," Mr. Fester said pitifully, bowing his head.

"Mr. Fester," Loyola cut in, putting their plan into play straight away. "You told us that you have a son."

"Yes," Mr. Fester said, wiping his eyes.

"Do you see him much?" she asked.

"Not as much as I'd like. He's busy with his three girls, and he runs his own business."

"What type of business?" Loyola asked.

"He has a craft studio. He makes his own pottery."

"Where's his studio?" she asked.

"He doesn't live here. He lives on the eastern shore in Lower Narrow Spit."

"I've been there," Loyola said. "That's where they have the annual lobster festival."

"That's right. It's this weekend. I'm going to visit him, and he wants me to check out the seniors' residence named Sunset Manor while I'm there."

"How long will you be gone for?"

"Hard to say. Will you keep a lookout for Buster while I'm away?"

Trevor cut in.

"Sure we will. Does your son know that Buster's missing?" he asked.

"No. Not yet. I was hoping Buster would come home before he found out."

"Maybe it's time to tell him," Trevor said gingerly.

He knew exactly what he was doing. If he could get Mr. Fester to confess about his long-dead dog to his son, his son would see that his dad was confused and shouldn't be living alone. And Mr. Fester would get the help he needed.

"You're right. It's time," Mr. Fester said, his shoulders sagging, his arms hanging limply.

"We better go exercise these dogs," Trevor said. "And we'll look out for Buster."

It was a lie. Trevor and Loyola both knew it.

Mr. Fester waved them off and stood forlornly at the door for the longest time.

"Do you think we did the right thing? Getting Mr. Fester to tell his son about Buster?" Loyola asked.

"That's the only way his son will see what's going on," Trevor said. "Besides, Mr. Fester must be really lonely. And that whole thing about finding playing cards with the queen wearing glasses that his wife tucked into used books? That's just downright sad. I can barely stand to think about it."

Loyola nodded along, but Trevor still felt uneasy, as if he was snitching on someone he cared about.

Poor Mr. Fester.

When Trevor and Loyola reported for duty at the animal shelter on the third Wednesday in May, it was Isabelle Myers who spoke first.

"Mr. Fester's been calling here every day from his son's house in Lower Narrow Spit, still looking for Buster. It's pitiful. I can't understand why we haven't come across that missing dog."

"There is no Buster," Trevor said flatly.

"What do you mean?" she asked.

"Buster died years ago. Mr. Fester is confused."

"Oh dear," Isabelle Myers said. "Well, that makes sense. We have a very good record when it comes to lost dogs. Eventually, they all show up here. Even strays."

"Not this time," Trevor said. "Does Mr. Fester's son know that he's calling you?"

"I'm not sure," Isabelle Myers said. "Perhaps I should ask to speak to his son the next time Mr. Fester calls, and then I can explain the situation."

"Good idea," Trevor said.

Not only was he getting Mr. Fester to rat on himself, he was now getting others to rat him out, too.

It was for Mr. Fester's own good, Trevor reasoned. So why did he continue to feel bad? Maybe he should bring it up with the lunch crowd back at Queensview. See what they thought.

"How's community service going?" he asked the boys the next day over sandwiches.

"I'm reading *The Case of the Waylaid Water Gun* out loud to a group of men who are losing their vision," Noah said, having been assigned to the hospital for veterans. "Only one old guy keeps interrupting. He wants to guess who's guilty before everyone else. Every time he shouts out a name, they all get into a great debate. I can hardly get a word in edgewise."

"You think you have it rough?" Miller said. "Try my job. I'm down at the used clothing depot sorting donated socks. Millions of socks. Why do people want their socks to match, anyway? Why can't we wear different socks on each foot?"

"You're just lazy," Craig said, still clogged up with allergies. "You'd never hack it at my job."

Craig delivered groceries to people who were stuck at home, or *shut-ins*, to use Craig's words.

"Who've you been delivering groceries to?" Trevor asked.

"Mostly people getting better from surgeries. My program is called Meals to Heal."

"Why is delivering groceries so hard?" Miller asked. "I run errands for my mom all the time."

"We're not talking about a dozen eggs or a bag of sugar, Miller. Shut-ins have to place one order to last them all week, so their grocery bags are really heavy and full of cans. Plus they all seem to live in third-floor apartments with no elevators."

"Well, I hate to break it to everyone, but I love my job," Bertram said.

The boys turned to Bertram, who volunteered at the soup kitchen.

"I get to write poems on the chalkboard about what's

being served for dinner. Just yesterday I was able to come up with a great one for sausage."

"How did it go?" everyone asked, including Trevor.

"I wrote, *We'll hold your taste buds hostage with our sweet Italian sausage.*"

"That's excellent," Trevor said. It was his turn. "I really like the animal shelter, too. Especially the dogs," he added, skillfully steering the conversation away from anyone mentioning Loyola.

"How many dogs do you walk?" Miller asked.

"Six altogether. But it's not the dogs that are hard to manage. I'm having a problem with one of the seniors."

"A problem?" Noah asked.

"He thinks his dog is lost, but he doesn't have a dog," Trevor said.

"I know what that is," Noah said. "It's called dementia. Elderly people sometimes get it."

"Not everyone gets dementia, though," Craig said. "My grandparents are fine."

"Mine, too," Miller added.

Bertram cut in.

"My grandmother had it. Her dementia got worse over time. That's why she moved to a seniors' residence."

"What's it like for the seniors who live there?" Trevor asked Bertram.

"They get excellent care," Bertram said. "And relatives can visit. Sometimes the residents with dementia know who their family members are. But sometimes they don't."

"They don't recognize their own family?" Trevor asked.

"Not always. That's why they can't live alone."

Trevor thought about Mr. Fester. Sad Mr. Fester with just his books for company and no dog. Trevor did not like the sound of dementia one little bit. The sooner Mr. Fester got help, the better.

Six

Sighting

It was now the end of May. Four more weeks of grade six. Four more weeks of community service duty. Four more weeks of walking the dogs with Loyola. And so far, not a single unpleasant comment about their heights had been made.

As Trevor headed to the animal shelter, it dawned on him that he might miss walking the dogs every Wednesday afternoon. He might miss Poppy with her insistence on pointing out every single bird they came across in the park. He might miss Misty with her ridiculous outfits. And for sure he'd miss Duncan with his trundling ways.

"What happens to the dogs when school's over?" he asked Isabelle Myers when he arrived.

"We're going to suspend the program over the summer. The seniors told us that they'd like to get out with their dogs themselves when the weather is warm."

"That makes sense," Trevor admitted. And then he realized he was getting worked up over nothing. His family was moving right after graduation, so he'd have to say goodbye to the dogs no matter what.

He'd have to say goodbye to his classmates, too. And to Loyola. That thought caught him off guard. Loyola? The giant? How things had changed. He didn't think of her as the giant anymore. He didn't even see her height. All he saw was the girl who sat with him at the park, told him funny stories about her family and wanted to be a librarian when she grew up.

But that was only when they walked the dogs. Back at school, Trevor and Loyola still kept a safe distance from each other. They both knew that if they were caught standing side by side with no dogs for distraction, the tired old comments would fly in their direction without fail.

Pipsqueak.

Half pint.

Munchkin.

Shrimp.

Squirt.

And all versions with the word *short*.

Shortstop.

Short stack.

Short stuff.

Shortcakes.

Shorty pants.

And for Loyola? Her labels were not much better.

Stretch.

Beanpole.

Giraffe.

Big Bird.

Palm tree.

Skyscraper.

And once, one that made her really cringe — Shorty pants.

Neither of them wanted to be targets if they could help it. And they could help it by staying away from each other.

After Loyola arrived at the animal shelter and they were putting on their safety vests, Isabelle Myers said, "Oh, I almost forgot!"

She pulled open the top drawer of her desk and took out a small red plush toy. It had black spots. She held it up for them to see. A ladybug. She squeezed it. It squeaked.

"Mr. Fester sent this," she said. "It was Buster's favorite toy. Mr. Fester wants you to carry it with you, if you could. He says that the toy still carries Buster's scent, and that Buster has a very good sense of smell."

"But Buster's dead," Trevor said, reaching for the toy just the same. "Were you able to talk to his son?"

"No, but his son must be taking care of things."

"What do you mean?"

"Mr. Fester stopped calling three days ago. But during his last call, he told me that his son had found a place for him at a seniors' residence near his son's house. He was moving in that day."

"What about all his stuff here?" Loyola asked. "His house? His books?"

"His son is putting the house up for sale. I guess he'll also arrange to move the rest of Mr. Fester's belongings."

"So that's it then. Mr. Fester is taken care of," Trevor said.

He should have felt relief. Instead, he felt uneasy. Something still wasn't quite right. Something was still niggling at him.

But what?

"Can I have that?" Loyola asked, pointing to the ladybug that Trevor was absentmindedly tossing back and forth between his hands. "I'm presenting my science project this week. It's about ways to get rid of pests in the garden without chemicals. Ladybugs get rid of them naturally."

"Sure," Trevor said, passing the toy to her.

She tucked it into her knapsack and they headed out.

Trevor pushed away all thoughts about Mr. Fester as he collected Misty, Duncan and Poppy. But when he came to Mr. Fester's house, he paused.

There was a big *For Sale* sign planted in the front yard.

The dogs automatically pulled in the direction of the walkway that led to Mr. Fester's front porch. They knew the routine.

"No," Trevor said to the dogs. "We don't go there anymore. Let's meet Loyola at the water fountain."

The three dogs looked at him with soulful eyes, and then they continued to the park with Duncan grumbling along the way.

Loyola was already there with her dogs.

"Did you see the *For Sale* sign?" she asked quietly.

"Couldn't miss it," Trevor said. He hesitated. He couldn't shake his sadness. "It's for the best, right?" he asked.

"I guess so," she said, but Trevor could tell she wasn't sure, either. She was just saying that to boost his spirits.

The way friends did.

And that did make him feel a bit better.

Lost in their own thoughts, they watched the dogs drinking fountain water.

"Ah! The children from the Queensview Mystery Book Club. We meet again."

Trevor and Loyola turned to see who was calling out to them. It was Edward Pond, the mystery writer who had once visited their club and who took walks in the park whenever he was stuck on his latest manuscript. He joined them at the fountain to watch the dogs.

"Are you stuck again?" Trevor asked.

"I'm afraid so," Edward Pond said. "My character can't decide what to do next. Should he board the express train and track down the art thief himself, or should he step aside and let the police botch the case yet again."

"Does your character own a gallery?" Loyola asked.

"No, my character is an artist. His paintings keep getting stolen from whichever gallery displays his work."

"Why?" Trevor and Loyola asked together.

"Ah," Edward Pond said knowingly. "The plot thickens."

Trevor and Loyola stared at him for further explanation.

"I still have to figure that out," he admitted, turning his attention back to the dogs.

"So you need to figure out the art thief's motivation," Loyola said with authority.

"Motivation? That's exactly right," Edward Pond said. "Good for you."

"We've spent a lot of time discussing motivation at our mystery book club," Loyola said.

"Motivation is key," Edward Pond confirmed. "And there are many types to choose from. Greed. Jealousy. Anger. Guilt."

"Guilt?" Trevor repeated. "Guilt is a motivation?"

"Oh, sure," Edward Pond said. "A very powerful motivation at that."

Trevor gulped. He knew he was feeling guilty about Mr. Fester. Loyola, too. Could their uneasiness be because the guilt they were feeling was motivating them to do something?

Maybe.

But Trevor had no idea what they should do. Mr. Fester was gone and so was Buster. And soon he would be gone.

"Does guilt go away on its own?" Trevor asked, glancing at Loyola and fearing the worst.

"Never," Edward Pond confirmed. "If anything, it only grows stronger. And it follows you everywhere. That's why it's such a powerful motivator."

Trevor instantly knew that Edward Pond was right. His guilt *was* becoming larger than life, especially with that *For Sale* sign planted in Mr. Fester's front lawn. Trevor felt a wave of panic. Suddenly, he was antsy to get a move on.

"Well," he declared in a falsely happy tone, "time to fly."

But he didn't need to prompt Loyola. She was already gathering up her dogs in her own guilty haste.

"See you again," Edward Pond said jovially as the two of them scrambled away with the dogs.

Trevor and Loyola marched down the path without a word, their guilt clinging to them like dark shadows. They said nothing during two poop breaks for Duncan and Scout. It was only when they rounded the third leg of the walk, past the bandstand with the domed copper roof and curling trellis for walls, that Trevor came to a full stop and broke the silence. He sat down on one of the green park benches that surrounded the bandstand. Misty and Poppy sat at his feet while Duncan practically collapsed on his side, his massive pink tongue hanging out, almost touching the ground.

"I feel terrible about Mr. Fester," Trevor confessed.

"I know. Me, too."

Loyola sat down beside him with her dogs.

"What should we do?"

"What *can* we do?"

"I have no idea."

"I'll tell you this," Loyola said, shifting the straps of her knapsack on her shoulders. "That little ladybug on my back just adds to my guilt. It weighs a *ton*."

MacPherson erupted into nonstop barking. They looked to see what was troubling him. Two teenagers were tossing a Frisbee on the other side of the bandstand. Each time the Frisbee soared in the air, MacPherson went nuts.

"Time to fly," Trevor said, "before MacPherson has a fit."

The rest of the walk was a glum affair all the way back to the animal shelter.

Trevor could not let go of thoughts about Mr. Fester.

"Did Mr. Fester sound okay?" he asked Isabelle Myers as they turned in their gear.

"Yes," she said. "He told me that he's very happy to be nearer to his son and his granddaughters. And he's already making new friends at the seniors' residence, including a widow named Laverne Bridge. The only thing is, he's still terribly upset about his dog."

"But there is no dog," Trevor insisted.

"Mr. Fester will be all right," Isabelle Myers said. "The dog is something he'll have to work out with the help of his son."

She pushed through the swinging doors behind her desk to put the safety vests away. The dogs in the back-room barked excitedly when they saw her. She came back and the barking stopped.

Trevor knew exactly how they felt.

Hopeful.

And then not hopeful.

Like Mr. Fester.

That week, stacks of flattened packing boxes and rolls of bubble wrap arrived at Trevor's house. With their checklists and tape guns and four label makers, moving had become a science for Trevor's family. They even had a fancy word for it. They *orchestrated* the move. And slowly, day by day, hour by hour, the things that Trevor loved the most — his toys from around the world, musical instruments and collection of globes — were packed into plain cardboard boxes or wrapped up in plastic.

"Great news!" Miller exclaimed during lunch on Friday. "My mom's booked the indoor go-cart track for my birthday party and you're all invited. The whole class!"

"The indoor go-cart track? That's awesome!" Noah practically shouted, for once at a loss for unusually big words.

"What's that they say on their commercials?" Craig asked, stuffed up as always.

"Get fast or get passed," Bertram rhymed off. "The course is supposed to have hairpins, tight corners and rapid straights."

"And don't worry about their height restrictions," Miller eagerly said to Trevor. "We checked and you'll be fine."

Trevor was both pleased and a little embarrassed, but he quickly pushed his feelings of embarrassment away. It was the indoor go-cart track, after all!

"I hear they post the fastest speed of the day, and whoever is the fastest gets a free pass for another visit," Trevor said. He could practically hear the roaring sound of the engines and smell the rubber tires. "When's the party?" he asked.

"July 10th," Miller said.

Trevor frowned. July 10th. He'd be long gone by then, unpacking in a house he'd never seen, halfway across the country, in a city he'd never been to. On to the next Big Adventure.

"What's wrong? July 10th is only six weeks away. I counted on the calendar this morning. It will go by in no time," Miller assured Trevor.

"I won't be here," Trevor explained matter-of-factly.

"Oh. Right," Miller said. He started to say something else, but changed his mind. Instead, he dug into his second chocolate pudding.

Bertram stepped in.

"We can send you pictures," he offered.

Trevor had heard promises like that before. How many times had former classmates told him they'd send letters and photographs? Only one or two of them ever followed through, and even that didn't last very long.

"I know it won't be the same thing," Bertram continued. There were awkward looks among the circle of boys.

They glumly dug into their food.

Trevor put them out of their misery.

"You know what they say," he said magnanimously. "Time to fly. New challenges and all that. Who wants some trail mix?"

He held open a plastic bag of his mom's homemade blend of pumpkin seeds, granola and dried apricots. All hands eagerly dug in.

"Hey, did you hear this morning's announcements?" Craig asked, picking a happier topic.

"The one about the time-capsule program?" Noah guessed.

Craig, Bertram and Miller nodded.

"What's the time-capsule program?" Trevor asked.

"The time-capsule program at Queensview is a very big deal," Noah explained. "Every seven years, someone in grade six is picked. At the end of the year, they get to fill their locker with whatever they want, and then that locker is sealed and a plaque is added."

"What types of things get put into the locker?"

"Anything they want. Stuff they made at school. Yearbooks. Sports equipment. You name it."

"I was in preschool when the last grade-six student was chosen. You were there, too, Miller," said Craig. "Remember?"

"A girl was picked, right?" Miller said.

"Yes, and she put in a giant water gun, an empty fish bowl and her snorkeling equipment."

"Why those things?" Trevor asked.

"In her speech she said that by the time her time capsule would be opened, fresh water would be scarce — only to be used for drinking and not playing around in."

"When does the time capsule get opened?" Trevor asked.

"Fifty years!" Miller said.

"Fifty years is a really long time," Noah said. "You should see the old guys at the veterans' hospital. I bet most of them are fifty!"

"Fifty years!" Trevor said. He whistled and shook his head.

Fifty years until the time capsule was reopened was practically forever. Then again, a mere six weeks to Miller's birthday was practically forever, too. Trevor wasn't going be around for either event. But he didn't let himself dwell on those sad thoughts. He took back his bag of trail mix and scarfed down the last of it.

Trevor was shutting his locker at the end of the day and was about to hoist his knapsack onto his back when he remembered that he had left his jacket by the school fence during the afternoon recess. It was his new dark blue one with the orange zippers and it fit him perfectly, not too long in the arms. His dad had brought it back from one of his flights overseas, and his mom would kill Trevor if he came home without it, so he charged out the back door of the school to the soccer field.

No one was around.

Trevor reached the fence line where he had left his jacket.

Only his jacket wasn't there.

Had someone taken it?

Doubtful. His jacket would be too small for most others to wear.

Had he left it somewhere else?

Trevor scanned the fence line on his left, and then he turned and scanned the right-hand side. Behind the fence was a back alley where the neighborhood houses kept their garbage cans and gardening sheds. He could smell a mixture of grass clippings and sour milk in the warm spring breeze.

He turned to scan the soccer field.

Wait.

There was his jacket, hanging from one of the soccer goalposts. Maybe a playground monitor had moved it there so that it would be easier for the owner to spot.

Trevor was about to leave the fence line when he heard a sound.

It was a familiar sound, a sound he was guaranteed to hear every Wednesday afternoon.

It was the happy sound of a dog shaking itself.

Trevor turned to the sound. He sucked in his breath.

It was a fleeting glimpse, the shortest of visions. It was there and then it was not there.

A dog. Certainly a dog. A dog with spots. A dog with spots shaking its head and body and then its legs. A dog with spots glancing at Trevor while turning a tight circle as if chasing its tail, then disappearing behind a row of garbage cans.

And then nothing.

Trevor stared in disbelief.

Surely he was seeing things. There wasn't really a spotted dog. There couldn't be. Mr. Fester's dog was long gone.

He stared and stared at the place where the spotted dog had disappeared, his heart pounding, his ears straining to hear something more.

But all he heard was the sound of children laughing in one of the backyards, a blue jay cawing like a squeaky clothesline and the distant roar of an airplane soaring high overhead.

Where was Loyola? He had to tell Loyola.

No. Wait.

Should he tell Loyola?

After all, he couldn't be sure of what he'd seen. Why get her upset?

Trevor waited some more.

The spotted dog did not reappear.

It was nothing, Trevor reasoned, backing away from the fence. I'm just out of sorts today because I'll miss Miller's birthday party, because I won't be around to see the opening of our class's time capsule in fifty years, because Mr. Fester still thinks he has a dog.

Trevor walked over to fetch his jacket, all the while convincing himself that he was seeing things.

And he was right.

He was.

That's why he didn't look back at the row of garbage cans.

Seven

More Sightings

ALL WEEKEND, Trevor was plagued by thoughts of what he had seen or not seen in the alley, while his parents continued to pack away the things that he would not see again until they had moved to their new place.

Those worrying thoughts about Buster made him cranky at every turn. He kept trying to pick a fight, but there were no takers. Both his mom and dad were in spectacularly good moods, because the prospect of moving again meant they were going to fly different types of airplanes, just the kind of experience they were looking for.

"Don't pack my kite," Trevor warned his mom as she headed upstairs with a stack of flattened boxes.

"Of course not," she said cheerily. "Not until the end, like always." She paused. "Is something wrong?"

Trevor shifted on the couch. He had been trying to read a new mystery book that Mr. Easton had suggested called *To Catch a Bicycle Thief*, but with all the goings-on around him, it was hard to concentrate.

"Can we get a dog when we move?" Trevor blurted.

He already knew the answer because he had asked a hundred times before, and the reply was always the same. So why bother asking?

Guilt. That's why. Edward Pond's lecture about motivation flashed in his mind.

His mom sighed. She leaned her stack of boxes against the stair railing and came over to sit down beside him.

"What's eating you?" she asked. "Not the move, is it?"

"No," Trevor said glumly, staring into his book without reading a word.

"Well, what then?" his mom insisted, gently closing his book.

"I just want a dog, that's all. I like the ones I'm walking each week, but none of them are mine."

"I'm sure you're taking great care of them," his mom said, skillfully preempting his usual argument that he'd take good care of a dog, so she needn't worry. "But we move too much and it's hard to rent a place that allows dogs. You know that, pumpkin."

Pumpkin. She always called him that when she had to tell him something difficult. Whenever he heard that nickname, he went straight to high alert. Unless she was offering pumpkin pie, which was his favorite dessert. Then he came running.

His mom made excellent pumpkin pie.

Suddenly he was hungry for pumpkin pie.

"Will you make me a pumpkin pie?"

"What? This weekend? I was planning to get ahead of the schedule by packing some of the kitchen."

Trevor knew the drill. The kitchen was always one of the last rooms to pack and one of the very first to unpack. That, and the beds. His mom usually baked a pumpkin pie almost as soon as they had settled. The smell instantly made the new house feel like home.

But if there was to be no pumpkin pie this weekend, Trevor went right back to trying to pick a fight.

"Miller's having a birthday party at the go-cart track and I'm invited," he said.

"That's wonderful," his mom said, falling into Trevor's trap. "You've wanted to try the track ever since we arrived. I'm sorry we didn't get a chance to take you ourselves."

"I'm not going," he said flatly.

"Why not?"

"It's in July."

"Oh," his mom said. She patted his knee. "You've really enjoyed your time at Queensview, haven't you?"

It was true. Trevor *had* really enjoyed his time. It was because of the people he had gotten to know. *Really* gotten to know. Mr. Easton. Mr. Fester. He paused. Loyola.

"Yes," he said glumly, making no effort to hide his feelings.

Even though he knew that the move wasn't his mom's fault — not really — he still wanted to punish her, because he suddenly realized that he was pretty sure he *had* seen a spotted dog in that alley and he had no idea what to do about it.

And he couldn't exactly tell her about that, either. What would he say?

Hey, Mom, I think I may have tricked an old man's family into thinking that he couldn't take care of himself because the old man had all this crazy talk about a spotted dog that doesn't exist, only there probably *is* a spotted dog, but too bad for the old man whose house is now up for sale.

"Tell you what," his mom said. "If I can get the winter clothes packed, I'll see about baking that pumpkin pie."

Trevor tried, but it was hard to stay mad at his mom who, despite being in the throes of yet another move, would stop to make him his favorite dessert.

"With whipped cream?" he asked, pushing his luck.

"Of course," she replied as she got up.

"Thanks," Trevor muttered. And then, "Where's Dad flying to today?"

"Winnipeg."

"How long?"

"Back tomorrow."

The doorbell rang.

"I'll get it," Trevor said, glad he was feeling better.

A doorbell usually meant some kind of package or delivery had arrived. But when he opened the door, it was Miller on the front porch.

"Some of the guys are meeting at the soccer field with their kites. Want to come?" Miller asked.

He was carrying his rolled-up kite which, when un-rolled, was the shape of a white box with a small red dot and a larger blue dot on it, and pointy black bits trailing on the corners. Miller said it was a Korean fighter kite, and it did look ominous, only Miller wasn't all that skilled at flying it. There were plenty of grass stains on the white bits.

"Mom, where's my kite?" Trevor bellowed.

"Still in your closet," she replied from somewhere inside the house.

"Be right out," Trevor said to Miller.

He rushed upstairs to his bedroom closet and pulled out his kite, which his mom had bought for him at a famous store called Sky High Kites on one of her trips.

It was an awesome kite. It was shaped like a Canada goose with a wind-inflated body and wings, a long black neck and black, white and brown markings. The only thing missing was the quack.

Both Trevor's parents were big kite fans. They each had their own kite. His dad's was in the shape of an orbiting satellite, and his mom's kite looked like an origami airplane made out of lined notepaper.

"I hope I have better luck today with the wind," Miller lamented as they walked along the sidewalk. "I don't think my kite is going to take many more crashes. Maybe it's just too heavy."

"I don't think that's it," Trevor said. "Airplanes are heavy but they fly."

"But isn't lighter better?" Miller asked.

"Not necessarily," Trevor said. "You need large wings to create the lift into the air to overcome the weight of your kite. But your kite must also be strong enough to take the force of the wind. So you need a balance. Light plus strong. Just like an airplane."

"Oh, that's right. Your parents are pilots. What's that like?"

"No big deal," Trevor said. "We get to fly for free. That's about it."

"I'd *love* to fly all the time," Miller said.

"When it's free, it's not so special," Trevor admitted.

"And you move a lot, too," Miller said.

Trevor could feel Miller tense up beside him. Miller was not the type who liked to talk about feelings or sad things or about anything that wasn't about to explode, burst into flames or crash in some hilarious way. Especially on such a blue-sky day.

"Hey! Is that Noah?" Trevor asked as they came onto the school's soccer field, changing the topic to something happier.

The wind was stiff, but not too stiff. Trevor got his kite up on the second try. Noah got his kite up, too, a blue-and-orange two-stick diamond kite with a long trailing tail of bow ties. The bow ties reminded Trevor of Mr. Fines.

When Craig arrived, he flew his delta kite with its triangular shape, extra batons for strength and keel. Craig could make his delta fly at really steep angles and swoop at the other kites. He was a menace.

Bertram was late on account of the shoe shopping he had to endure with his mom, during which she made him try on one hundred pairs, none of them as comfortable as the sneakers with holes he was still wearing. Bertram didn't own a kite, so Trevor let him fly his from time to time.

Meanwhile, Miller repeatedly crashed his Korean fighter kite to the point of no repair. Holding bits and pieces in his hands, he turned to Trevor.

"Can I try yours?" he asked.

"You're joking, right," Trevor said, his eyes glued to his goose in the sky.

But his eyes weren't always glued to his kite. Not entirely.

Every once in a while, he glanced at the back alley beside the soccer field where he thought he may have seen a spotted dog the day before. The alley remained ordinary in every way.

Rows of garbage cans and recycling bins.

Bikes leaning against garden sheds, abandoned in haste.

Sheets and pillowcases pinned to sagging clotheslines, snapping in the wind.

No spotted dog.

Suddenly, a crash rang out. It sounded like a metal garbage can lid hitting the pavement.

Trevor nearly let go of his kite.

"What was that?" he demanded.

The other boys barely shrugged, way too busy with their kite flying to care about a garbage can lid.

"Here," he said to Bertram, handing over the reel for his kite, "but keep clear of Miller."

Bertram happily took hold.

Trevor cautiously made his way over to the fence line. His heart was racing and his mouth went dry. What was he about to see?

Nothing, apparently. Nothing that had made that crashing sound, anyway. Just the breeze blowing in his ears. For all Trevor knew, that crashing sound might have even come from inside one of the houses, now that everyone was keeping their windows open to let in the warm spring air.

"What are you doing?" Bertram called to Trevor.

"Just seeing something," he called back.

"Seeing what?"

Trevor hesitated. What, exactly, should he say? The thought of telling the boys about the spotted dog, about the old man that he may have betrayed, about the terrible guilt he was feeling was too hard for words.

And then a wave of anger hit him. How did this happen? Why did he care so much? What made him get so involved?

Trevor made a vow then and there. When he moved, he would return to his standard routine — try new things, join new groups, but don't get to know anyone too well. Or look what happens.

"Time to fly," he muttered to himself.

"Miller wants a turn on your kite," Bertram called out.

Miller was standing right beside Bertram, grabbing at the string.

Trevor turned to the boys.

"Hold on," he called back, and strode in their direction, refusing to take a backward glance at the alley.

When Trevor arrived home after the kite flying, his dad met him at the door. He was in his uniform and on his way to Winnipeg.

"I'll be back tomorrow morning," he told Trevor and kissed him on the forehead. "Save a piece of your mom's pumpkin pie for me for breakfast," he added.

"I will," Trevor said.

Trevor liked his pumpkin pie warm, right out of the oven, but his dad liked his pumpkin pie cold from the fridge. He said that pumpkin pie tasted even better the next day.

Or maybe that was just how his dad had gotten used to eating it, flying around so much that he was rarely home when the pie came out of the oven. Trevor couldn't be sure.

His dad pulled out his car keys and headed down the steps.

"Hey, Dad?" Trevor said.

His dad turned.

Again, Trevor hesitated. Should he tell his dad about the spotted dog?

Trevor knew his dad didn't mean to, but he jiggled his keys, a sure sign that he was in a hurry to go. There was an airplane with its passengers waiting, after all.

"Safe travels," Trevor said, his standard goodbye.

"Roger that," his dad said, giving him a salute.

He climbed into his car, and Trevor went inside the house.

"Smells great, Mom," he called out.

The air was thick with warm cinnamon, nutmeg and brown sugar. And while Trevor ate his large slice of still-warm pumpkin pie with extra whipped cream, he almost forgot about the spotted dog that he may or may not have seen.

Almost.

But not quite.

It was the first Monday morning in June. Trevor and the rest of the grade-six class sat cross-legged on the shiny wood floor of the auditorium, all staring up at the stage. There Ms. Albright, the school secretary, stood holding a large basket. Inside the basket were the names of each and every grade-six student written on folded slips of paper. Mr. Easton was swirling his hand in the basket, making a big deal out of picking one single name.

The students buzzed in anticipation.

Mr. Easton plucked a slip of paper from the basket and held it up for all to see.

"And the Queensview Elementary student chosen to be this year's time-capsule participant is …"

He unfolded the paper and read the name. Then he held the piece of paper out for Ms. Albright to read. She smiled.

"Trevor Tower!"

Whoops and cheers flew all around Trevor with lots of thumps on the back and friendly shoves.

"Congratulations, Trevor!" Mr. Easton exclaimed.

Trevor beamed. He had never won anything before. Or if he had, he had never stuck around to hear the results.

"What are you going to put in your time capsule?" Noah asked as everyone stood to go back to class, now that the selection was over.

"Don't know," Trevor admitted. "I'll have to think about it."

With each family move, Trevor had worked hard not to leave anything behind. It was strange to think that this time he could fill a locker with whatever he wanted, and the contents would be safe in one place for fifty years.

Trevor caught Loyola's eye as everyone went up the stairs toward their classroom. She gave him a quick nod and a slight smile, nothing more. Their pact remained in place at school, despite his good fortune.

But their pact was about to be broken for good. Later that day at lunch, while chasing after a stray soccer ball, Trevor saw the dog with spots. This time there was absolutely no mistake. It was sitting alongside the school fence, watching the game.

Trevor froze, forgetting the ball, which rolled right past the dog.

"Buster?" he called tentatively.

The dog cocked its head to one side.

"Is that your name?" Trevor asked, trying hard to keep his voice even.

The dog thumped its tail on the ground. Twice.

The only thing that separated Trevor and the dog was the long fence. He knew that there was no way he could climb over that fence without frightening the dog away.

But if he couldn't get to the dog, he could at least get to a witness.

Loyola.

"Stay," he said to the dog as calmly and as firmly as he could.

Trevor slowly backed away, then turned and tore across the soccer field as fast as his legs could carry him.

"Trevor, get the ball!" a few players called out in confusion.

Trevor ignored them. He rushed inside the school in search of Loyola.

She wasn't in the library with Ms. Wentzell, or in the lunchroom with the chatties, and she definitely was not in the gym with the basketball players.

"Have you seen Loyola?" he kept asking everyone he came across.

All he got were shaking heads or shrugged shoulders.

He ran into Mr. Easton near the teachers' lunchroom.

"Have you seen Loyola?" he asked, almost completely out of breath.

"She's waiting for her mom on the front steps of the school," he said. "She forgot her lunch."

"Thanks," Trevor said, and he was off.

He rushed down the hallway and yanked open the front door. Startled, Loyola looked up from her step, a mystery book open on her lap.

"Loyola," he said. "You need to come see this."

"See what?" she asked nervously, while others eyed them curiously as they slowly passed by.

"A spotted dog," he said, ignoring everyone except Loyola.

"A spotted dog?" she repeated softly, closing her book.

"I think it's Buster."

"You think it's Buster?" she repeated, eyes widening.

"I'm pretty sure," he said.

Loyola gulped.

"Where?" she asked.

"By the fence on the soccer field."

"Are you certain?"

"Come and see."

"I can't go now. My mom's coming with my lunch."

"When?"

"Any minute."

Trevor looked up and down the street. There was no sign of Loyola's mom.

"Tell you what. You go check out the fence line. I'll stay here and keep a lookout for your mom."

"You mean it?" she asked.

"Yes, but hurry. The dog might not stay there for long."

Loyola nodded and ducked into the school, the quickest way through to the back door and the soccer field.

Trevor stood on the steps anxiously waiting for Loyola's return.

Would she also see Buster or would she be too late? And if she did see Buster, then what? Should they catch the dog and return it to Mr. Fester? No, that wouldn't work. Mr. Fester had moved to a seniors' residence. Trevor was pretty sure that seniors' residences did not allow dogs. And he couldn't take the dog. His family moved too much.

What about Loyola? Could she take the dog?

A woman on a bicycle pulled up to the front of the school. She locked it to the bicycle rack, then headed to the steps. She was carrying a blue camouflage-patterned lunch bag. It was the same blue as the tables in the school's cafeteria. Loyola's need to blend into the background knew no bounds!

"Are you Loyola's mom?" Trevor asked her.

"Yes, I am," she said, pausing on the steps.

"I'm Trevor. She wanted me to take her lunch for her."

"Trevor from the animal shelter?"

"Yes."

"How nice to meet you! Loyola has been telling us all about her adventures with you and the dogs."

"She has?"

"Oh, sure. Let's see. You have Misty and Duncan and Poppy. She has Scout and Ginger and …"

Loyola's mom tapped her helmet, trying to remember the name of the last dog.

"MacPherson," Trevor said.

"That's right. MacPherson, who hates Frisbees. She tells us that your favorite dog is Duncan."

"I like Duncan," Trevor admitted. "He's a good bulldog, but not much of a walker."

"I can imagine. So where's Loyola?"

Trevor hesitated. Should he tell her about his Buster sighting? Loyola's mom had mentioned every other dog but that one. Perhaps Loyola had been keeping just as quiet at home as Trevor had been about Mr. Fester and his lost dog. If that was the case, he wasn't about to break the news to Loyola's mom now. Friends didn't tattle on each other. He knew that much.

"Loyola's on the soccer field," he said, which was true enough.

"The soccer field?" her mom said. "That's unusual. She's not much into sports."

"What about equestrian?" Trevor said, and he smiled despite his worry about Buster.

"Ah, you've heard her standard joke," Loyola's mom said. "I like that one, too."

She studied Trevor, and he shifted his feet. Was Loyola's mom about to tell him that *he'd* make a much better jockey, joining the long list of others who had something to say about his height?

She held up Loyola's camouflaged lunch bag.

"Would you please be sure she gets this? I need to get back to work."

"I will," Trevor said, and he happily took the lunch bag from her.

Loyola's mom was all right.

"Do you have a dog?" he blurted just before she turned away.

"No, we don't. Our condominium board won't allow it."

"Oh," Trevor said, disappointed at having to rule out Loyola's family as a potential home for Buster if they ever caught him.

He stood watching as Loyola's mom unlocked her bike, then pedaled down the street after giving him a friendly wave goodbye.

Moments later, Loyola pushed through the door of the school and stood staring at him. It was hard to read her face. Was she confused? Shocked? Horrified?

"So?" he demanded.

"I didn't see it," she said simply.

"You're kidding," Trevor said incredulously. "It was right there by the fence."

"I didn't see it," she repeated, taking her lunch bag from him.

"Did you look all up and down the fence line?" he challenged.

"Yes. It wasn't there."

This was infuriating. Trevor knew what he had seen. He was sure of it this time.

"Well, it certainly *was* there. I saw it. It had spots and everything. Exactly how Mr. Fester described."

"I went as fast as I could," Loyola said apologetically.

"Oh. So you believe me, then?"

"Of course I do."

Trevor nodded with relief.

"What now?" Loyola asked quietly.

"I have no idea," he admitted.

Loyola sat down on the steps and opened her lunch bag. She pulled out a sandwich and unwrapped it — plain cheese, same as Trevor's favorite, but this was not the time to mention that happy coincidence.

Between bites, Loyola said, "I'm sure you saw a spotted dog. What we need to do now is make sure that the spotted dog you saw is actually Buster."

Her observation hit him like setting off the metal detector at an airport security gate.

"That's brilliant!" Trevor exclaimed. "There must be hundreds of spotted dogs in the world. I'm getting worked up about nothing."

Loyola's theory made perfect sense. Mr. Fester's dog couldn't possibly be alive after all these years. Mr. Fines said so. Isabelle Myers, too.

"Tell you what," she said, wiping her mouth. "I still have Buster's favorite toy, remember?"

"The stuffed ladybug?"

"Yes. The science fair is over. I'll grab the toy from my locker after school and drop it over the fence where you last saw the spotted dog. If the toy goes missing, or better still, if you see the spotted dog again and it's carrying Buster's toy, then we'll know for sure."

It was a good plan.

A smart plan.

A simple plan.

"I like your plan," Trevor said. "I like your plan a lot."

The plan was so perfect, he was comforted by it.

Two days later, after the boys ate their lunch, they rushed to the soccer field for a quick game. Trevor was chasing the soccer ball when it bounced off the fence.

And there, behind the fence, watching the game, sat a spotted dog. The ball startled the dog, and it turned to bolt down the alley.

But not before it grabbed the stuffed ladybug that was lying between its front paws.

Eight

——

No Dogs Allowed

"It *is* Buster," Trevor said to Loyola as soon as she entered the animal shelter that afternoon.

"Why? Is the ladybug missing?" Loyola asked, rushing her words.

"Yes, and the spotted dog has it," Trevor confirmed. "I saw it again at lunch, and this time it took the toy."

They both stopped talking and turned to Isabelle Myers.

Isabelle Myers had been on the telephone ever since Trevor arrived for duty. She was still on the phone, talking to someone about the animal shelter's adoption program.

They turned back to each other.

"Do we tell her?" Loyola said under her breath.

"I think we have to," Trevor said. "Mr. Fester was her client. And, well, he deserves to know."

Loyola nodded sadly. They waited anxiously until Isabelle Myers hung up the phone.

"Good to see you both," she said cheerfully, getting up from her desk.

She was about to retreat to the back room to get their safety vests when Trevor stopped her.

"I think we've seen Mr. Fester's missing dog," he blurted.

"Who, Buster?" she asked.

Both Trevor and Loyola nodded.

"Where?"

"By the school. Behind the soccer-field fence," Trevor said. "Three times this past week."

"And why do you think it's Buster?"

"It looks exactly like how Mr. Fester described his dog. And it has Buster's ladybug. We left it out by the fence, and now that dog is carrying it around."

Puzzled, Isabelle Myers slowly sat back down at her desk. She opened a drawer, fished around and pulled out a calculator. She punched in some numbers.

"Okay, look," she said. "Mr. Fester said that he took Buster with him to work each day at the used bookstore he owned."

"That's right," Trevor said.

"How old was Buster then?"

Trevor thought back to what Mr. Fines had told him.

"Fifteen years," he reported.

"And I remember the year that Mr. Fester sold his

bookstore. In fact, he donated dozens of animal-care books to us when he sold it. So, if we take this year, minus the year he sold the bookstore, plus the age of Buster at the time the bookstore was sold, it equals …"

She held the calculator out for Trevor and Loyola to have a look.

"Twenty-four," Loyola said.

Both Trevor and Loyola grew quiet.

"Here's what I'm thinking," Isabelle Myers continued in a gentle voice. "Sure, you saw a spotted dog, and sure, that dog took the toy. But it just can't be Buster. The average lifespan of a dog that size is only thirteen to fifteen years."

"So you're saying there's a stray dog out there who looks and acts exactly like Buster?" Trevor said.

"Yes, that's my theory," Isabelle Myers said, putting away her calculator. "Sadly, there's no shortage of stray and abandoned dogs."

Trevor nodded. He knew that Isabelle Myers was trying to make him feel better, but he couldn't shake his niggling feeling that there was something not quite right about her theory.

Trevor pictured the dog by the fence. Okay, it had spots. Lots of dogs had spots. Okay, it grabbed the ladybug. Lots of dogs liked stuffed toys. Trevor thought some more. He gulped. He remembered calling out Buster's name. What did the dog do then?

Thumped its tail.

Twice.

As if it had just heard its name.

Barking erupted and Trevor looked up to watch Isabelle Myers disappear through the swinging door to the back room. The barking stopped when she returned with the safety vests.

Lonely, desperate barking.

"All set?" she asked brightly, handing them the safety vests and the walkie-talkies.

"The bags," Loyola quietly reminded her.

"Oh, that's right," she said, grabbing a handful of plastic bags from her desk and dividing them between Trevor and Loyola.

Once outside, but before they went their separate ways to pick up their dogs, Trevor said, "I can't explain it, but I'm sure about what I saw. I'm positive it was Buster."

Loyola nodded sadly.

"Let's talk when we get to the park," she said, and she strode to her side of the street before Trevor could argue.

That disappointed him. After all these weeks, they still weren't comfortable walking together, not without the dogs for distraction.

"Hello, Mrs. Tanelli," Trevor said when she answered her door.

Misty sat politely beside her, a big grin on her face.

Trevor bent to give her an ear rubby while Mrs.

Tanelli retrieved her jacket and pink leash.

"Come here, you," she said to her dog.

Misty obediently pulled away from Trevor and stood for her jacket. This time the print on the jacket featured the Eiffel Tower, French bread, black berets, bricks of cheese, a bottle of wine and two glasses crossed at the stems, croissants, fancy high-heeled shoes, snails, a painter's palette, and a French poodle that had been trimmed so that it had pom-poms on its ears and ankles and one its tail. The jacket also had the words *Oh-la-la* and *I love Paris* on it.

"My sister sent this back to me from France," Mrs. Tanelli explained, buttoning Misty. "She spends her springs there."

"It's nice," Trevor said, which was true. It certainly beat the panda bear and leopard outfits Misty had been wearing.

"Have a lovely walk," Mrs. Tanelli said. *"Au revoir!"*

Trevor took the pink leash and walked down the street to Duncan's house.

"Let's go see Duncan," he teased Misty. "You remember him, don't you?"

Misty grinned like a maniac as she pranced along beside him.

"Hello, Mrs. Ruggles," Trevor said when she answered her door.

"Come in, Trevor," she said.

He stepped inside.

Mrs. Ruggles adjusted her gigantic, thick glasses and studied Misty through the glass door. She made a *tut-tut* sound.

"Duncan won't be impressed by that European designer outfit," she said. "He's a home-grown boy who doesn't go for fancy world travelers and showy airs."

Trevor doubted that Duncan would be impressed by anything.

"Where is Duncan?" he asked.

"Duncan! Walkies!" she called out gaily.

Somewhere deep inside the house they heard a *hurrumph*.

"Duncan hasn't been himself today. The vet has made me put him on a diet. You don't think he's too fat, do you?"

"No," Trevor said politely.

But he wasn't sure. Duncan was as wide as he was long, and with all the wrinkles and his enormous head, it was hard to tell what was muscle, what was fat and what was just plain bulldog.

"Duncan! Come!" Mrs. Tanelli called again.

Duncan rounded the corner, pink tongue hanging to the side. He plowed up to Trevor and stood for his leash, looking defeated.

Or maybe not defeated. Again, it was hard to tell.

Misty paced anxiously outside.

"All set?" Trevor asked Duncan.

Duncan did not look up.

"Excellent," Trevor said. "Me, too."

They headed out.

Misty tried her level best to get Duncan's attention as they made their way to Poppy's house.

Duncan, as usual, devoted all his mental powers to the task of looking straight ahead and walking at his unhurried pace.

"Hello, Mr. Fines," Trevor said at Poppy's door, shouting above Poppy's hysterical barking.

"Poppy, sit! Poppy, sit! Sit! Sit!"

Poppy finally composed herself, but not without the occasional whimper of happy anticipation.

"I'll go fetch her leash," Mr. Fines said once she had settled down somewhat.

Poppy shook her head in excitement. Her ears helicoptered above her.

"Seen any interesting birds?" Trevor asked her as bits of spittle flew against the hallway wall.

Poppy scooted over to Trevor and sat down on top of his feet. She looked straight up at him with moist brown eyes and a joyful grin, her stubby tail wagging against the polished wood floor.

Mr. Fines came back to attach her leash, bending down stiffly to do so.

"I was wondering about something you told me," Trevor said.

"And what was that?" Mr. Fines said, slowly straightening up.

"You used to go to the bookstore called A Likely Story."

"I did indeed," Mr. Fines said. "I still go from time to time, but it isn't the same as when Heimlich Fester owned it. The selection isn't as good. Too much fiction. Not enough naval history. At least they kept the seniors' discount."

"You mentioned that Mr. Fester had a dog that used to work with him at the bookstore," Trevor said.

"Yes. Buster."

"What did Buster look like?" Trevor asked.

"Oh, I don't recall, exactly. That was a few years ago. Quite a few years ago now."

"He had spots, right?" Trevor said, hoping to prompt Mr. Fines' memory.

Mr. Fines reached down to pat Poppy.

"Yes, spots, short ears, medium-sized." Mr. Fines thought some more. "And as I said, Buster loved movie scripts. Specifically, romantic comedies."

"Romantic comedies?" Trevor repeated dubiously.

"That's what Heimlich claimed," Mr. Fines said. "Frankly, I think he was the one who loved that genre. Buster was a cover-up. If I were to hazard a guess, I dare say that Buster was more of an action or spy thriller kind of dog."

"Where did Buster hang out in the bookstore?" Trevor asked.

"Buster had a bed in the window of the store, near

the front door. He loved to watch the street traffic when he wasn't napping or being read to."

"Did Buster have a favorite toy?"

"A favorite toy? Like a chew toy or a bone?"

"Yes, that kind of thing. Or something softer."

Trevor knew from all the mystery books he read that he was leading the witness.

"Something softer?" Mr. Fines repeated.

"Sure. Like a stuffed toy."

"A stuffed toy?"

"Like a ladybug or something."

Trevor was starting to feel very foolish, and Poppy was beginning to pull at her leash, anxious to get on with their walk.

"He may have. The dog had quite a collection of toys. Customers were always coming across them on the bookshelves. They'd bring whatever they found up to the cash register when they were making their purchases, and then Buster would grab the toy and hide it back on a shelf somewhere. It was a little game, something Heimlich's wife especially enjoyed."

Mr. Fines paused. "I see that Heimlich's house is up for sale."

Trevor nodded. "He's gone to live at a seniors' residence near his son."

"I'm glad to hear it," Mr. Fines said. "I was starting to worry about him, especially after you told me he thinks Buster is lost. He became quite lonely after his wife died. And then he sold his bookstore. He even quit his long-standing volunteer organization."

"Which one was that?" Trevor asked.

"The Twillingate Cemetery Brigade."

"With Mr. Creelman?" Trevor asked.

"You know him?" Mr. Fines asked.

"Not really," Trevor said. "He came to my school's mystery book club."

"Whatever for?"

"He talked about reading clues on gravestones at Twillingate," Trevor said. "Are you also a member of the Brigade?"

"Good heavens, no," Mr. Fines said. "I wouldn't be caught dead spending all that time in a graveyard." He smiled at his little joke.

"Good one," Trevor said, suddenly excited because Mr. Fines had given him a new lead. "Well, we'd better head out."

When Trevor arrived at the park fountain with his three dogs, he floated his new idea by Loyola.

"I've been thinking. Instead of going around the park today, how about we walk the dogs somewhere else."

"Like where?" Loyola asked.

"The cemetery."

"The cemetery? You mean Twillingate?"

"Yes."

"Why?"

"Poppy's owner, Mr. Fines, just told me that Mr. Fester used to volunteer for the Twillingate Cemetery Brigade, so Mr. Creelman might be able to confirm that there is no Buster."

"Maybe. But we're talking about Mr. Creelman. We're the reason he didn't get any volunteers this year."

"I know. But he was also the one who suggested that we complete our community service duty at the animal shelter. I bet he likes dogs."

"This Buster thing is really bothering you, isn't it?" Loyola said.

Trevor nodded and looked away. In fact, he felt terrible.

"I've never been inside the cemetery," Loyola said. "Have you?"

"No."

"Remember Mr. Creelman's talk? All those stone carvings? All those creepy skulls and crossbones. They were really frightening."

"I thought they were for dead pirates," Trevor admitted.

"Me, too. Boy, did we get *that* wrong."

Loyola laughed, and then she instantly sobered.

"What about the ghost?" she asked.

"You've been talking to Miller," Trevor said.

"Not just Miller. Everyone knows about the dead husband who's looking for his wife's name."

"Actually, that's a perfect excuse. Let's see if we can find that grave marker, and while we're there, we might run into Mr. Creelman."

Loyola studied her dogs, who were all having a drink at the fountain. She looked down at the clothes she was wearing. Lots of dark grays and deep greens. She'd blend into the cemetery perfectly.

"Would we walk there together?" she asked quietly.

Trevor frowned. The pact. He had almost forgotten about it. He thought some more. It wasn't like they'd be walking together down the street alone. They'd still be walking the dogs. And if no one was saying anything about their heights in the park, they weren't likely to say anything along Tulip Street, which would lead them to Twillingate.

It was worth the risk.

"We'll have the dogs," Trevor reminded her. He didn't have to say anything more than that. He knew she'd know what he meant.

She nodded.

They gathered their dogs, but it wasn't easy. Poppy was confused at the change of plans and kept trying to turn back to the park where there were birds. Scout kept a suspicious eye on them the whole time, while sniffing at the ground constantly, as if memorizing their new route in case they got lost. And Duncan had to be coaxed to move at all, probably thinking that he might end up walking longer than usual. He kept coming to a full stop every single time he got the chance. Trevor had to ply him with cookies from the box that Mr. Fester had given him, which he still had in his knapsack.

So much for the diet.

And then, just as they were closing in on the iron gate of the cemetery, a group of daycare children walked by. There were eight little ones all holding onto a rope while toddling along in a row with two daycare workers, one at the front leading the way and the other at the back, making sure there were no stragglers. They were singing "Row, Row, Row Your Boat." The children immediately broke rank when they came across the dogs.

"Doggies! Doggies!"

Trevor and Loyola patiently waited until everyone in the group had a turn patting their dog of choice.

"Wrinkles! Wrinkles!" the little ones said, patting Duncan's head.

"Soft! Soft!" they said as they stroked Poppy's long silky ears.

"Little! Little!" they said, bending down to scratch MacPherson's back.

Scout seemed especially patient with them as they tugged at his giant bushy tail.

"Okay, children," the lead daycare worker declared. "Let's get going. It's almost snack time."

"Cookies! Cookies!" the little ones chanted, which got the dogs excited all over again.

They fell into line, taking their places along the rope, and they toddled off down Tulip Street.

Trevor and Loyola gathered their dogs and walked the remaining half block to the front gate of the cemetery, which was open. They stood to read the ominous signs:

Beware of Falling Gravestones
Enter at Your Own Risk
Closed at Sunset
No Dogs Allowed

"No Dogs Allowed," Loyola said out loud.

"Let's tie them to the gate. We won't be long and Scout will warn us with a bark if something's wrong," Trevor suggested.

They tied the dogs. Ginger got a triple knot. Scout stood guard.

"I don't see Mr. Creelman," Loyola said, scanning the cemetery.

Rows upon rows of lichen-spotted grave markers faced them with their grim symbols of death. Some looked as if they were about to fall face first onto the damp grass, some already had, and some had epitaphs so badly eroded, the words were impossible to read.

"I'm sure he'll be along," Trevor said. "Let's see if we can find the double grave marker that's blank on one side."

They walked along the entire first row by the fence,

searching for the grave that Miller said haunted the cemetery. The names on the gravestones were unremarkable, and the descendants of many of them attended Queensview Elementary.

McDougall, Lynch, Chisholm, Thomas, Stairs.

"Here it is," Trevor exclaimed. *"Pettypiece."*

They stood before a thin gray gravestone, which had two sets of angel heads and wings carved at the top. The man's name, Enoch Pettypiece, and the dates of his birth and death were filled in on one side, but curiously, the other half remained blank, just like Miller had described. The grave marker also went on to read that Enoch had lived to be 33 years, 5 months and 8 days old, and that *He was an affectionate husband, tender parent, lived respected and died lamented.*

"Look!" Loyola said, pointing to the word *affectionate.*

It had a carved box around it, as if the word had been changed or reworked. Maybe Miller was on to something after all.

"That's odd," Trevor said, bending down to take a closer look.

But as he did, a shadow swept across the words, making it harder for him to read.

"Can I help you?" a gravelly voice said from behind him.

Loyola gasped and Trevor nearly jumped out of his skin. He spun around and leaped back at the same time, almost knocking down the old grave marker.

It was Mr. Creelman in his orange coveralls. He looked as stern as ever, despite his comical bushy white eyebrows. He carried a shovel.

"Careful," he warned.

"Hello, Mr. Creelman," Trevor said as soon as he recovered.

"How do you know my name?" he demanded, narrowing his eyes.

"You came to our school," Trevor reminded him. "The Queensview Mystery Book Club."

"I lectured on symbols," Mr. Creelman recalled.

"That's right," Trevor said warily, saying nothing about the other time he had met Mr. Creelman at the public library.

"Were you paying attention?" Mr. Creelman asked. It was more an accusation than a question.

"I think so," Trevor said doubtfully.

He hoped Loyola would jump into the conversation, but she was doing her shrinking-into-the-background thing and was standing as still and as silent as the grave markers around her.

"Then what does this mean?" Mr. Creelman demanded, pointing the tip of his shovel to the angel heads with wings on the top of Pettypiece's gravestone.

"They're angels," Trevor said, which he immediately regretted, for surely this was a trap, just like all the other questions Mr. Creelman had asked during his visit to the Queensview Mystery Book Club.

"Wrong!" Mr. Creelman declared triumphantly. "Dead wrong! This is a soul effigy. It is the most common symbol found on Twillingate's gravestones dating from the mid-eighteenth century to the mid- to late-nineteenth century. They began as variations of death heads — like the early skulls and crossbones — and evolved into something resembling angels. Angels were later replaced by the Greek revival symbols of the urn and willow."

"Oh," Trevor said flatly, hoping this would not encourage an expanded lecture.

"Scholars have written extensively on the reasons for the evolving artistic interpretations. Some think it is due to the shift from Puritan fire-and-brimstone ideas to a more worldly Age of Enlightenment perspective. The early death head warns visitors that they must live every moment in anticipation of death and transition to the afterlife, which would bring an eternity of either salvation or damnation. But the angel-type figures — soul effigies — herald the Romantic or Victorian times and a more optimistic outlook in terms of the hereafter. They are glorified souls, not grim reminders of inevitable death."

Trevor looked around and spied other soul effigies.

"Some of them look happy," he observed. "And some of them look mad."

"That's because the carvers were uncertain about their own eternal fate," Mr. Creelman said sourly. "I covered all this at Queensview." He turned to Loyola. "Why are there six dogs tied to the gate?"

"Those … those are ours," Loyola stammered.

"Yours? All six?" Mr. Creelman demanded, interrogation-style.

"Well, not really," Loyola said. "We're dog walkers. And the sign at the gate said *No Dogs Allowed*."

"Oh, I see. You're the two who didn't want cemetery duty. I recognized *you* from the public library," he said, glaring at Trevor.

Trevor said nothing. His guilt spoke volumes. Loyola tried to shrink some more.

"Then that must be Mrs. Ruggles' bulldog," Mr. Creelman said. "Looks like she's still spoiling Duncan with too much food."

"She has him on a diet," Trevor said, feeling the weight of the box of dog cookies in his knapsack.

"And I see you must have Poppy. How is Mr. Fines?"

This was just the invitation that Trevor was hoping for.

"Mr. Fines isn't good," he said. "He's worried about Mr. Fester."

"Heimlich Fester? We've all been worried about Heimlich for years now. He's never gotten over the death of his wife. And selling his bookstore? Big mistake."

"He claims he's lost his dog," Trevor said.

"Who? Buster?"

"Yes."

"That's a shame. I'll keep a lookout. Buster likes to come in here from time to time."

"Wait! What? Isn't Mr. Fester confused? Buster died a long time ago."

"Not the one he owns now," Mr. Creelman said. "He's still a pup."

Trevor stared at Mr. Creelman, struggling to take in the enormity of his words.

"What do you mean? There really *is* a Buster?"

"Of course there is. He took in a stray dog almost a year ago. Named him Buster after his first dog. Goes everywhere with him. That's why he had to quit volunteering for the cemetery brigade. No dogs allowed."

"A stray dog?" Trevor repeated.

"And cagey. The vet told him Buster must have been living on leftovers in garbage cans and compost bins for months. Took Fester ages to get the dog used to people."

"What does Buster look like?" Trevor dared to ask, even though he already knew the answer.

Mr. Creelman didn't hesitate.

"He's spotted, just like the first one," he said, his words tossed out like shovelfuls of dirt, digging Trevor's grave.

Nine

—

Queensview Mystery Book Club

TREVOR AND LOYOLA gathered the dogs at the gate of the cemetery in silence and headed down Tulip Street without a word. It was only after they passed the stone public library with its stained-glass windows that Loyola finally spoke.

"Do you think Mr. Creelman will catch Buster?" she asked.

"I don't know. Maybe he will. Him or someone else from the Twillingate Cemetery Brigade," Trevor said. "But even if they do, Buster will still end up at the animal shelter. Mr. Fester won't be able to keep his dog at the seniors' residence now that he's moved for good."

They walked the dogs past Queensview Elementary before speaking again. The only sounds were the occasional grunts from Duncan and the jingle of the medals of bravery dangling from Scout's collar.

"And soon you'll be moving, too," Loyola said, even more quietly than before.

"Yes," Trevor said.

"Have you sold your house?"

"We rent," he said. "We move too much to own. Renting makes moving easier."

Loyola nodded. She didn't look at Trevor.

"I don't mind moving. I'm used to it," he said, guessing her thoughts.

He knew how this conversation went. He had had it with classmates many times in the past. It seemed easier on them if they thought he was happy about moving. And when they thought he was happy about the move, they would change the subject to something else, something Trevor felt like discussing. It always worked like a charm.

"And this time I get to leave something behind in a time capsule, although I don't know what yet," he added, a further attempt to cheer her up.

He glanced at Loyola, but his words didn't seem to have the effect he hoped for. Instead of changing to a new topic, she kept quiet. They didn't speak another word until they returned to the animal shelter after dropping off the dogs to their homes.

"There really *is* a Buster," Trevor confessed to Isabelle Myers when he handed over his gear. "We ran into Mr. Creelman, and he told us that Mr. Fester took in a stray puppy about a year ago. He named it Buster after the dog that had kept him company all those years at the used bookstore."

"Oh dear," she said. "Poor Mr. Fester."

Trevor and Loyola nodded glumly.

"Well, if Buster turns up here, I'll be sure to call Mr. Fester. I've kept his telephone number."

"But Mr. Fester won't be able to keep Buster at the seniors' residence," Loyola said.

"No, but at least he'll know that Buster is safe. And we'll work hard to find his dog a good home. I can promise him that," she said.

Trevor could tell that she had said the standard line about finding a good home many times, just like he said his standard line about time to fly. They were both trying to reassure others.

Only sometimes their lines didn't work.

"See you next week," he barely replied.

"It's a beautiful day," Mr. Easton announced that Friday at the beginning of their language arts class. "How about we take our books outside to the soccer field to read?"

The students whooped, Trevor included. Everyone headed outdoors.

The class scattered across the field, each student choosing a spot on the soft new grass. They cracked open their books and read by the sunlight, which burned warm on their backs. Other than birds singing and the occasional squeaking clothesline, there were no interruptions for the next half hour. Then Mr. Easton gathered the class near the goalpost to read another chapter of *The Science Fair Incident*. It was the part where a backyard rocket launch goes terribly wrong.

Trevor leaned back on his elbows, his legs outstretched and his eyes half-closed, listening to the story. Mr. Easton was an excellent reader. He would change his voice when he spoke the dialogue from different characters, and he knew exactly when to pause, making the story extra suspenseful.

Mr. Easton read until almost the end of class, and when he closed his book, he said, "Looks like we have an extra student today."

Trevor opened his eyes and sat up to see what Mr. Easton was talking about.

All eyes in the class were turned to the fence beside the soccer field. Trevor followed their gaze.

Buster was sitting on the other side of the fence listening to the story, his head tilted, the stuffed ladybug at his feet. When he noticed that the reading had ended and that all the students were now staring at him, he grabbed his toy and bolted down the alley.

Trevor gulped. He looked over at Loyola. She sadly shook her head.

The same thing happened the following Tuesday morning when Mr. Easton offered to hold his class outside again. It was another blue-sky day with not a single cloud. The softest breeze occasionally fluttered the bright white pages of their books as the students read.

This time Trevor kept a lookout for Buster, and across the soccer field, in another spot, Loyola was doing the same thing. Neither of them got much reading done. But when Mr. Easton gathered the students by the goalpost to read out loud the latest installment of *The Science Fair Incident*, Trevor fell into a pleasant trance, eyes half-closed, taking in all the details of the story as he floated against the blue sky. It was only when Mr. Easton closed his book at the end of class that Trevor came back to earth and spotted Buster.

Once again, Buster sat by the fence with his toy listening to every word as if he enjoyed Mr. Easton's company just as much as the students.

When the reading ended, Buster disappeared on cue, but not before Mr. Easton noticed him in the audience.

Trevor lingered on the field to see if Buster would reappear as the rest of the class went back inside the school. He waited until he and Mr. Easton were the last ones to leave.

"Your family must be getting ready for the move," Mr. Easton said to Trevor as they headed in.

It was just like Mr. Easton to care about what was going on with each of his students.

"Yes. Pretty much everything is in boxes," Trevor said. "My parents are very efficient."

"I could use some packing tips," Mr. Easton said. "I'll be moving, too."

"What? Where?" Trevor asked.

"My hometown. Ferndale."

"But you just got here," Trevor said, who remembered that Mr. Easton had arrived at Queensview at the start of the school year, the same as he had.

"I know. And I'll miss this school very much, especially the students. But Ferndale's my hometown. And there's someone back there whom I hope to marry."

"Oh," said Trevor, at a loss for words.

He was surprised at how sad he felt, more sad than he really should be. After all, he was leaving Queensview Elementary, too. What difference would it make if Mr. Easton remained there or not?

Then Trevor realized something. He had always liked to comfort himself with the thought that whenever he moved, he could always go back to the school and that it would be exactly the same, including the people he had left behind.

With Mr. Easton moving, that comforting thought was gone. Queensview Elementary would never be the same, not without Mr. Easton. It made Trevor's move feel much more permanent.

"I wonder who that dog belongs to," Mr. Easton said as they neared the back door of the school.

"The dog with spots by the fence?" Trevor asked guiltily.

"Yes. I've seen it hanging around school lately."

"You have?" Trevor asked, slowing his pace.

Mr. Easton nodded. "When we read outside, and other times, too. I sometimes see it when I stand at the classroom window." He held open the door for Trevor and added, "I don't think it's a stray."

"Why not?"

"It wears a collar. It also carts around a toy. I think it's lost."

"Lost?" Trevor repeated, his heart thumping in his chest, making it difficult to hear.

"Maybe you should mention it at the animal shelter the next time you report for duty," Mr. Easton suggested as they headed up the stairs to the second floor. "See if that dog's owner has reported it missing."

"Good idea," Trevor managed to say, his guilt stopping him from spilling Buster's miserable story to Mr. Easton.

Just before they got to the door of the classroom, Mr. Easton turned to Trevor.

"Please don't mention my move," he said. "I'll make that announcement to the class at the end of the day."

"They're going to be sad," Trevor said.

"I know. But I've got a wonderful last assignment for them, and you can help."

"How?"

"Have you thought about your time capsule? About what you'd like to put in it?" Mr. Easton asked.

"No, not really," Trevor admitted.

Trevor surprised himself. When he was first chosen, he had been so excited by the idea of leaving something of himself behind at Queensview besides appearing in a few photographs for the yearbook. But with all his worries over Mr. Fester and Buster, he had mostly forgotten about the time capsule.

"Well, I have an idea. Can you lend me some space in your locker?"

"Sure," Trevor said. He smiled at the honor. "What for?"

"I'll give you the details at the end of the day."

Trevor nodded happily. The sting of Mr. Easton's move had been lessened. He took his seat in the front row. But before Mr. Easton sat at *his* desk, he paused at the classroom window and scanned the fence line.

"Do you always eat the same thing for lunch?" Bertram asked Trevor as they sat at a table and unwrapped their sandwiches.

Everyone except Miller. As usual, he started in reverse order by first peeling back the lid of his chocolate pudding and digging in.

Trevor studied his plain cheese sandwich and shrugged.

"My life's a constant change," he said. "So I like to know I can depend on lunch."

"How's the move going?" Craig asked through his stuffed nose. His allergies were getting worse, now that they were well into spring.

"The same as all the other moves," Trevor said. "Time to fly," he added automatically. He took a bite of his sandwich and chewed.

He was still thinking about what Mr. Easton had in store for his locker, so the next bit of conversation caught him completely off guard.

"I saw the strangest thing in the cemetery as I was walking by this morning," Bertram said. He leaned in as if he were about to tell a ghost story around a campfire. The only things missing were a starry night and him holding a flashlight up to his face.

And the campfire.

The other boys stopped eating their lunches to listen.

"Where? Twillingate?" Trevor asked, catching up to the conversation.

"Of course it was Twillingate," Bertram said. "This town has only one cemetery."

"Oh. That's why it's so big," Trevor said.

"Was it the ghost?" Miller jumped in. "The one from the double gravestone with the missing words?"

"Epitaph," Noah corrected.

"Sure. Epitaph. Was the ghost wandering around?" Miller asked eagerly.

"No. It wasn't a ghost. It was Mr. Creelman," Bertram said.

"Mr. Creelman? So what? He's a volunteer ground-skeeper there," Craig said. "Along with all those other old guys. The Twillingate Cemetery Brigade."

"I know that," Bertram said. "But he was by himself, and he was behaving very strangely."

"How do you mean?" Miller said.

"Well, he was crouching behind gravestones and darting between them. Kind of like he was spying on something. Something up ahead."

"Spying? What would he be spying on?" Craig asked.

"A ghost!" Miller announced. "I'm telling you! There's a ghost in that cemetery. Everyone says so."

"I didn't see a ghost," Bertram insisted. "But I think something else was there. Only it was small. Smaller than the gravestones, anyway, because I couldn't see it from where I stood on the sidewalk."

Trevor forced himself to ask.

"Was it a dog?"

"A dog? Maybe. But why would he be sneaking up on a dog?"

"There are no dogs allowed in the cemetery," Craig said. "There's a big sign posted at the gate."

"Well, maybe that dog couldn't read," Noah said, smiling at his own joke.

"I'm telling you. It was the ghost," Miller insisted. He turned to Bertram. "Then what happened?"

"I came to school."

"That's it?!" Miller asked.

"What do you mean, 'that's it?' Mr. Creelman was sneaking around the cemetery. That's very strange, don't you think?"

Miller polished off his chocolate pudding looking very disappointed about no ghost.

Trevor could hardly take another bite of his sandwich. Mr. Creelman had spotted Buster. He was certain of it. He was trying to catch the dog. But then later that morning, Trevor had seen Buster by the school fence. So Mr. Creelman had been unsuccessful.

Would Buster ever be caught? Would he ever find another home? Or would Trevor be forced to move away without knowing the fate of the spotted dog? That thought was unbearable.

Trevor had to act. He had to do something to help Mr. Creelman catch Buster.

But what?

Then he remembered Buster by the school fence, sitting and patiently listening until Mr. Easton finished reading out loud. Just like the first Buster, this dog seemed to like being read to. If Mr. Creelman knew that, maybe he could read in the cemetery and lure Buster to him.

"Excuse me," he said to the others, and he went back to his classroom early, most of his lunch uneaten.

Trevor dug out a clean sheet of paper from his desk and wrote a note to Mr. Creelman in his best handwriting. His plan was to tuck the note into the gate of the cemetery after school on his way home. Mr. Creelman would be sure to find it the next time he entered the cemetery with the rest of the Brigade on one of his missions.

Dear Mr. Creelman, Trevor wrote. *Buster likes to be read to, just like Mr. Fester's first dog. Maybe you could read out loud in the cemetery. It might be easier to catch Buster if you did.*

Trevor read over his note. There was still plenty of white space. He thought he should add one more line of encouragement.

Maybe you could read your book of epitaphs, like you did at the Queensview Mystery Book Club, he added, hoping that flattery might work.

There was still a bit more white space. And Trevor desperately needed to clinch the deal.

He thought back to when Mr. Creelman had visited their school with his blue bin of cemetery stuff and had finished off the class by reading one epitaph after another. Trevor recalled that there was a nice section of epitaphs written especially for pets. There was one in particular about a Dalmatian who had served as a heroic fire-station mascot.

Trevor wrote, *Maybe Buster would like the one about the fire-station mascot, because it was about a spotted dog, too. Sincerely, Trevor Fowler.*

Trevor read his note again. Satisfied, he carefully folded it and put it in his knapsack to be delivered later that day.

It was almost the end of the last class of the afternoon, the late-day sun shining through the window, when Mr. Easton made his announcement. He started off by telling the students how much he had enjoyed his year with them, and how they had taught *him* rather than the other way around. Then he dropped his news.

"I'm going to be leaving Queensview Elementary and moving back to Ferndale."

There were soft gasps all across the room.

"I've been offered a teaching job there, and, well, Ferndale is where I grew up. I miss my hometown very much."

Trevor didn't nod in agreement because there wasn't a single place that he had lived long enough to call his hometown. But everyone else in the classroom seemed to know exactly what Mr. Easton was talking about. Their surprise quickly turned to sympathy.

"Will you finish out the school year with us?" Loyola asked from the back of the room.

"Absolutely," Mr. Easton said. "And before the school year ends, I have one more assignment for you."

Everyone held their pens at the ready, waiting to take notes.

"I would like each of you to write a short story, a true

story, something that really happened to you during your time at Queensview. But I want it to be a story about a situation where something went wrong, something that you never got a chance to fix and may never get the chance to make right."

"Like what?" Miller asked.

"Well, maybe you broke something at home and let your little brother or sister take the blame. Maybe your pet died and you never got the chance to say goodbye. Maybe you borrowed something very precious from a friend and then lost it. That kind of thing."

Noah said, "So you're talking about an autobiography."

"Isn't that like a diary? My sister has one," Miller said. He turned in his seat to face the rest of the class. "Only hers has a lock," he added bitterly.

"Your sister has the right idea," Mr. Easton said. "And like that diary with the lock, I won't be reading your stories. In fact, no one will be reading your stories. That's where Trevor's time capsule comes in."

All eyes turned to Trevor.

"What I want you to do is write about something difficult. Then you'll put your story into an envelope and seal it. Trevor has agreed to provide space in his time capsule where you'll put all your stories. And there they'll be stored, safe and secure, for the next fifty years."

"So we'll be writing something that no one else will read?" Craig repeated in awe. "Not for fifty years?"

"Exactly," Mr. Easton said. "That's the most important part, so you'll need to keep this in mind as you're
writing. That way you can be truly honest. And if you
can be truly honest now, it will make you a much better
writer for other projects." He paused. "There's one more
thing. By writing about a bad situation, you might find
that you'll feel better about it, even though you still
can't fix the problem. So if there's one particular thing
that's troubling you the most, you should probably
write about that. After all, you'll never get a chance like
this again."

Mr. Easton had been pacing back and forth at the
front of the room while he spoke, but then he made his
way over to the window. He took a moment to scan the
fence line before returning his attention to the class.

The students grew silent, pondering the assignment.

Trevor had no trouble whatsoever coming up with
what he would write about.

Ten

―――

A Likely Story

WHEN TREVOR stepped outside after the last class of the day, a warm almost-summer breeze brushed against his face. Others bumped past him as he opened his knapsack. His note to Mr. Creelman was still there.

He knew that coaching Mr. Creelman on how to capture Buster was a good idea, but he couldn't help feeling out of sorts.

It was guilt.

It had to be the guilt.

Maybe he should go back inside, see if he could track down Loyola. She might go with him to keep him company.

But, no. She wouldn't go with him — not without the dogs. Despite all their time together during their community service work, despite all the talks and all the laughs, even despite the trouble they were in now, he knew that she wouldn't want to be seen walking alone with him. That's how much she hated the tall jokes. And if Trevor was truly honest with himself, he hated the short jokes just as much.

What a shame. For once, Trevor had spent enough time with someone to almost form a true friendship. If only their heights hadn't been such an obstacle.

Trevor took a deep breath and headed down the steps of the school on his own. But as he walked along the sidewalk, he was filled with feelings of regret. Up ahead, on the right, he could see the beginning of the ominous iron fence that surrounded the ancient cemetery, its bleak gray markers sprouting up from the bright green spring grass. But a bit beyond, on his side of the street just before the florist's shop, was a large colorful sidewalk sign with the word *Sale* written in cheerful handwriting. It was placed in front of the used bookstore called A Likely Story.

Mr. Fester's old store.

Trevor had never been in there before, and his curiosity won him over. He passed the cemetery and ducked inside.

Ink. Ink and dust. That's what he smelled. And something familiar that reminded him of the animal shelter. Lasagna?

"Don't mind me," a voice floated toward him. "I haven't had my lunch yet."

Trevor stood uncertainly at the door. He had a hard time locating the owner of the voice among the enormous clutter and the stacks and stacks of used books crammed next to each other from floor to ceiling. There was barely any place to walk between the sagging, overstuffed bookcases. And there were far too many top shelves for Trevor's liking.

"Come in, come in!" the voice merrily called out.

And then Trevor spied her — a young woman wearing an elephant-print scarf and black triangle-shaped glasses. She came out from behind the camouflaged desk to greet him. She was wearing polka-dot tights and holding a take-out carton from Sacred Grounds Cafe, fork poised over a thick slice of cheesy lasagna.

"Sacred Grounds Cafe makes the best," she said, pointing to her lunch with her fork.

"I heard that," said Trevor, realizing he was hungry because he hadn't eaten much of his own lunch that day on account of writing the note to Mr. Creelman.

"What can I do for you?" she asked.

"I'm not sure," Trevor said hesitantly.

And he wasn't. He had no real reason to be in the store, other than stalling his visit to the cemetery. He tried to make up something.

"I'm here to buy a gift," he said in haste.

"Lovely! For who?" she asked.

"Um," he said in an attempt to think of someone's name and coming up empty. He was still out of sorts.

"Oh. I see," she said and smiled slyly at him. "A girl."

"Right," Trevor said. He knew a girl. "Loyola," he said.

"Loyola. What a pretty name."

"I guess," Trevor said. He had never thought about it.

"Tell me about Loyola," she said.

"I don't know. She's in grade six? She likes dogs?" His statements came out sounding more like questions.

"Lots of girls like dogs. Tell me something specific about Loyola so that we can find the perfect book for her. Something unique that she's interested in."

"Something unique?" he repeated.

Trevor thought back to when he started community service duty with Loyola and the first time they discovered that they actually had something in common.

"Loyola likes solving puzzles," he said triumphantly, remembering their conversation in the park.

"Perfect!" she exclaimed, setting down her lunch on her desk. "Come with me."

Trevor followed her as she zigzagged through the maze of books toward the back of the store. They came to a section with a sign hanging overhead that read, *Detectives and Mysteries*. Then she started running her finger over the spines of the books on the shelves below the sign, reading the titles to herself.

"No. No. No," she kept saying, before moving onto another row. And then, "Ah! Here we are!"

She pulled out a bright yellow book and handed it to Trevor. The front cover featured a boy secretively passing along a note to a girl while they were sitting in a classroom. He read the title out loud. *"How to Crack Codes, Ciphers and Other Secret Messages."*

Trevor opened the book to flip through the pages. Each chapter started with a story, and then sprinkled throughout the chapters were plenty of diagrams that showed codes, signals, ciphers, sign language and invisible writing. The blurb on the back read, *A fun-filled book about codes and secret writing used during real world events.*

Loyola might actually like this book, he thought. He certainly would. He checked the price, which was handwritten on the inside cover. Did he have enough money? Trevor reached around and set his knapsack on the ground. He opened the small outside pocket where he stored whatever was left of his allowance. He counted the money. Not quite enough.

He must have looked sad, or crestfallen as Noah would say, because the store owner said, "No worries. That's close enough. It's for a girl, after all." She beamed at him.

Trevor shrugged. He was happy to get a good deal. He walked with her to the front counter, which was also covered with stacks of books, to pay. As he was sliding his purchase into his knapsack, he remembered something unusual about the used bookstore.

"Do you ever come across playing cards tucked into some of the books?" he asked.

"Why, yes, I do," she said with astonishment. "Always the queen."

"Are they wearing a hand-drawn pair of glasses? Red glasses?"

Her eyes widened even more.

"Yes!" she exclaimed. "What do you know about them?"

"I met the previous owner of this store. His name is Mr. Fester."

"Yes, that's right. Heimlich Fester. I bought the store from someone who bought it from him years ago."

"Well, he had a wife who loved to play cards. She was in tournaments and everything. He nicknamed her the Queen of Bridge. Anyway, before she died, she tucked playing cards with the queen into books throughout the store, just to remind him of her."

"Oh my! What a beautiful love story!" she said, surveying her inventory in awe.

Trevor shrugged again and turned to go.

"I hope your special friend enjoys the book," she said, returning to her lasagna.

"Thanks," Trevor said as he found the door.

He crossed the street and headed back down the sidewalk to the gate of the cemetery. As he walked along the iron fence, he scanned the grounds for any signs of Mr. Creelman. There were none. Trevor set his knapsack down to fish out the note that he had written. He spotted it jammed between Loyola's book and a pad of paper with Mr. Easton's description of the last assignment written inside. He plucked the note out and wedged it between the decorative curls of the open iron gate. He heard something that made him look up.

A bark.

He scanned the cemetery. A gray sea of silent gravestones faced him with their eroding names and dates. The only movement came from the birds overhead, flitting from treetop to treetop, and a squirrel who scolded him from the top of the gate. Then he saw a dog.

Just a glimpse.

By the first hedgerow, under a bench.

The dog had spots.

"Buster," Trevor called, his heart pounding.

He took a tentative step inside the cemetery. Then another step. Then another. Pretty soon he was well inside, past the first ten rows of headstones, past the double grave marker with one side missing its epitaph, and headed in the direction of where he last saw Buster.

Now he was well past the oldest section of the cemetery with the ominous skulls and crossbones plastered everywhere, and he wandered into the newer section filled with white marble sculptures. Many of the headstones were deeply carved with angels or had statues of figures in mourning, weeping into their hands or looking sorrowfully up at the sky. One of them had the carving of a small lamb resting on top, its little head of curly wool tilted slightly as if it was watching passersby. A child's grave marker.

Trevor reached out to touch the lamb's head. It was warm from the sun.

He pressed on, feeling bold. Now he was in the newest section of the cemetery, with rows and rows and rows of polished granite gravestones lined up with precision. These were much smaller, much less elaborate than the marbles and more squat, but the names and dates were deeply carved in razor-sharp letters, and they gave him the feeling that they would last forever.

Trevor also noticed that some of the rows had gaps, places where people had bought a plot but were not yet buried. Way off to his right, at the end of one of the rows, was a fresh mound of soil without grass. A recent burial. Trevor walked toward it and saw bouquets of wilting flowers arranged at the base of the grave marker. He could also make out the epitaph. It read, *Only in darkness can you see the stars.*

Trevor didn't want to get too close, but that wasn't what stopped him. He had stumbled across a stuffed toy ladybug lying on the grass between two granite rows. Trevor picked it up. It was still damp from being held in a dog's mouth.

"Buster?" he called.

But Buster was nowhere to be found, probably having already doubled back and escaped through the front gate. All Trevor heard was the sound of the birds in the trees, and, way off in the distance, the engine of a jet airliner flying overhead. He put the toy in his knapsack.

"Good afternoon, young man," said a gravelly voice behind him.

Trevor whirled around and came face to face with Mr. Creelman in his orange coveralls holding a grass trimmer. Trevor's mouth went dry.

"Did you leave this for me?" Mr. Creelman held Trevor's note up with his gnarly fingers. His tone was accusatory.

"Yes," Trevor said, trying very hard not to sound so nervous. "I … I'm worried about Buster. About finding a good home for him."

Mr. Creelman's face softened, but only a little. Then he scowled again.

"I've already tried reading out loud. Hasn't worked so far."

"Did you read from your book of epitaphs?" Trevor asked.

"Yes," Mr. Creelman said matter-of-factly, shoving the note into the pocket of his coveralls.

"Is Buster here often?" Trevor asked.

"Comes and goes," Mr. Creelman said.

"Does he look hungry? I have a box of dog cookies," Trevor said eagerly, desperate to help. He was about to set his knapsack on the ground and fish out the box, but Mr. Creelman stopped him.

"Already have cookies," he said, arms crossed, hugging the grass trimmer handle to his chest, not giving Trevor an inch.

"Oh," Trevor said, deflated and out of ideas.

"It's not a matter of catching him," Mr. Creelman said. "It's a matter of what to do with him after he's caught. Heimlich can't take him at the seniors' residence, and his son's children are highly allergic to dogs, so Buster can't go there, either. That's why he's been begging everyone to find Buster a new home."

Trevor gulped. Poor Buster.

"Can you take him?" Mr. Creelman asked, giving him a level glare.

"Me? I'd really like to," Trevor said, and he meant it. "But my parents are pilots and we move around too much to own a dog." Then he added, but not as cheerfully as he would have liked, "We're about to move again, right after school ends."

"You're moving?" Mr. Creelman asked, eyebrows raised.

"Yes. This weekend, actually. Everything is in boxes."

"Must be tough," Mr. Creelman said. His face softened once again, but only a little.

Trevor usually made some comment at this point in the conversation about liking change so as to brighten the mood, but this time he couldn't manage it. He looked at Mr. Creelman, with his bushy eyebrows and the deep lines around his mouth, and then he looked around the gloomy place and declared, "I hate moving."

Even as the words came out, he was surprised. He was telling the truth for once. He had no reason to pretend with Mr. Creelman. And it felt good to confess.

"Most don't," Mr. Creelman said, "but not everyone."

"I guess you're right," Trevor said. "Our teacher, Mr. Easton, is moving back to Ferndale and he seems happy about it."

"I know. I ran into him at the public library, returning all his books and paying his overdue fines. If he keeps up with his writing and teaching, he's going to need someone to help organize him."

"I think there's someone in Ferndale he wants to marry," Trevor said.

"Yes. So I've heard." He paused and then he shot his hand up in the air in a way that told Trevor to stop talking.

They both stood frozen, Trevor having no idea why.

Then, after a long moment, Mr. Creelman slowly lowered his hand to his side.

"Thought I heard Buster," he explained.

Trevor looked around. No Buster. Just headstones.

"What about that girl you hang out with?" Mr. Creelman said.

"Who? Loyola?" Trevor asked.

Mr. Creelman nodded.

"What about her?" Trevor demanded, surprising himself for the second time in the conversation. Why was he feeling so protective of Loyola?

"Could she take Buster?" Mr. Creelman asked.

"Oh. I don't think so," Trevor said, standing down. "She lives in a condominium. No dogs allowed."

"Hurrumph," Mr. Creelman said, sounding like Duncan. "Well, I have to get back to work." He repositioned the grass trimmer in both hands. "This cemetery doesn't take care of itself."

Trevor felt bad about bailing out on cemetery duty. And now Mr. Creelman was the only person who might be able to help him catch Buster and put his mind at rest before he left this place for good. He took a step toward Mr. Creelman.

"About that," Trevor said. "Maybe Loyola and I should have volunteered with the Twillingate Cemetery Brigade after all."

"What do you mean?"

"It's because we volunteered with the Pet Patrol that Buster doesn't have a home."

"I don't follow."

"We didn't believe Mr. Fester about Buster. And now he's moved to the seniors' residence because no one believed him."

"I see," Mr. Creelman said, scowling all the more.

"So maybe we would have been better off here," Trevor said, his voice trailing away, "cleaning gravestones and not interfering with living things and all."

"What about the other dogs?" Mr. Creelman said.

"The other dogs?" Trevor repeated.

"You've been walking all those other dogs. Who would do that if you weren't volunteering at the animal shelter?"

"No one, I guess," Trevor admitted.

Mr. Creelman took a deep breath and slowly let it out. He rubbed his stubbly face with his gnarly, yellow-stained fingers. He cleared his throat.

"Trevor," he said, less gravelly than before. "Those dogs deserve good care. All dogs do." He shrugged. "Life is for the living. Don't you ever forget that, no matter what the future throws your way."

Trevor looked at Mr. Creelman, who stood surrounded by grave markers with the words on the bottom rows covered by tall grass that needed trimming. But that's not what he would remember when he thought back to this day. Trevor would remember Mr. Creelman's advice, which brought him enormous relief now, and would bring him relief many times down the road, move after move after move.

As Trevor left the cemetery, he decided he would stop by the public library across the street, where he first learned about dog breeds, to complete his last assignment. He called home as soon as he arrived.

"Don't be too late," his dad advised. "Your mom's flying in around five."

"I didn't know she had a flight today," Trevor said.

Even the fridge calendar with their flight schedules — always one of the last household items to be packed — had been boxed up.

After Trevor made the call, he settled at the table underneath the stained-glass window with the Twillingate Cemetery Brigade plaque. The sunlight coming through the window was spectacular — jewels of ruby red, indigo blue, pumpkin orange, grass green and lemon yellow. He dug out his notebook and a pen and opened to a fresh page.

Then he wrote his opening line: *This is a story about Buster.*

When Trevor arrived at the animal shelter for the last time, Loyola was already there. They put on their safety vests, grabbed their walkie-talkies and some plastic bags, then headed out, Trevor still on his sidewalk, Loyola on hers, a wide-open street between them. It was a cloudy day, cooler than the day before when Trevor had met Mr. Creelman at the cemetery.

Trevor caught up to Loyola and her dogs at the water fountain, just like always. This time none of his dogs tried to pull into Mr. Fester's yard. It was as if they could read the brand-new sold sign.

"Nice outfit," Loyola said as Trevor's dogs took their drink.

She wasn't talking about Trevor. She was talking

about Misty, who was sporting a purple jacket with a feather boa around the neckline. Her toenails were also painted purple.

"Yes, Duncan certainly thinks so," Trevor said.

He, Loyola and Misty all looked at Duncan.

Duncan didn't even flinch at the mention of his name. He had planted himself in the shadow of a nearby tree, his enormous tongue doing its usual thing. He was staring at the path ahead of him, completely oblivious to Misty.

"I'm going to miss Duncan," Trevor admitted.

"Me, too," Loyola said. "I'm going to miss all the dogs."

Silence followed, and what Trevor really wanted to say next was, "I'm going to miss you, too."

But he couldn't. He wasn't brave enough. And besides, he'd never said that to anyone before.

Instead, he thought that maybe he would give the book in his knapsack to her now.

No.

He wasn't ready to say goodbye. So he avoided looking at Loyola, all the while hoping she might say that she would miss him.

"We'd better get going," Loyola said, cutting into the silence, and they gathered their dogs.

As they walked along the outside path, Trevor noticed that the dogs had not changed one bit since they first started walking them. Poppy was always on the hunt for birds, her long ears perking up whenever she heard a caw or a chirp. MacPherson was continually scanning the skies for incoming Frisbees. Ginger was always hanging back plotting her escape route. And Scout never let up casting Trevor a look of suspicion, as if to say, "You're not fooling me, young man."

Both Trevor and Loyola gave the dogs extra cookies all along the way, knowing that this was their last walk together and ignoring Duncan's diet. In fact, Trevor emptied the box. The dogs enjoyed the extra attention, unaware they would not be seeing Trevor or Loyola again.

It would be nice to be a dog, Trevor thought with envy. But then he realized that it would be nice to be a dog only if the dog had a good home.

Buster.

Poor Buster.

"Thanks ever so much for your help," Mr. Fines said when Trevor dropped off Poppy. "You've been brilliant."

Trevor scratched behind Poppy's ears and under her soft jowls before he turned to go. "Stay away from the birds," he joked as he headed out the door.

"Poor Duncan," Mrs. Ruggles said. "He's going to miss you."

Trevor gave Duncan one last pat on top of his wrinkled head. Duncan stood patiently for his goodbye.

When the patting ended, he waited a bit longer, then grunted before trundling off to the kitchen for a nap after his long walk. Trevor could hear him collapse with a *hurrumph*.

"Misty has so enjoyed her play dates with Duncan," Mrs. Tanelli said. "You've been very kind. And now that the weather has improved, I'm looking forward to taking her out myself in our matching outfits."

Misty sat on his feet and smiled up at him, her purple boa floating all around her face.

"Goodbye, Misty," Trevor said. "You're a real show-stopper."

Trevor felt choky as he left Misty's house. He tried to shake it off as he walked, but his throat only got tighter as he neared the animal shelter. Why was this feeling so strong? What was so different? He'd never felt so sad about any of his previous moves. He took a deep breath and opened the door, the bell announcing his arrival.

Isabelle Myers must have been in the backroom with the animals, because she wasn't at her desk. Loyola was the only one in the waiting room. Together, they took off their safety vests and placed their walkie-talkies on her desk without a word. But they could hear voices behind the swinging door.

Trevor and Loyola stood awkwardly by the desk. They knew they should wait until she came back out so that they could say goodbye. The muffled voices behind the door continued, along with a laugh. A man's laugh.

Trevor looked at Loyola and Loyola looked at Trevor. They had heard that laugh before. But where?

The swinging door pushed open. Out came Isabelle Myers, followed by Mr. Creelman. Only Mr. Creelman wasn't the one who had been laughing. It was the younger man who came out last.

Mr. Easton.

Mr. Easton walking with a spotted dog on its leash.

A spotted dog named Buster.

Eleven

Last Assignment

"You've found Buster!" Trevor and Loyola exclaimed.

"And a home for Buster, too," Mr. Creelman growled.

"You're going to adopt Buster?" Trevor asked Mr. Easton.

"Looks like it," Mr. Easton said happily. "He'll move with me to Ferndale. And I've promised to bring him by to visit Heimlich Fester from time to time. Ferndale is quite close to Lower Narrow Spit where he now lives."

"How did you catch him?" Trevor asked Mr. Creelman.

"I called up Heimlich. He told me I was going at it all wrong. Instead of reading out loud something Buster liked, which kept him alert and full of beans, he told me to read something that put the dog to sleep. Then all I had to do was clip a leash on his collar. Simple."

"What did you read?" Loyola asked.

"Heimlich suggested *A Bridge Player's Handbook*, specifically the chapter on winning no-trump leads. I own a copy."

"That would certainly put Mr. Fester to sleep," Trevor said, turning to Mr. Easton. "He didn't like bridge, but his wife was excellent. She used to play with Mr. Creelman."

"Never lost a tournament," Mr. Creelman said. "We were great at camouflaging *and* sacrificing queens."

Mr. Easton bent down to scratch Buster's head. Trevor and Loyola knelt to pat his back. He was a muscular dog and his fur was short and wiry, but his ears were very soft. Buster wagged his skinny tail.

"We'll just need to complete some paperwork," Isabelle Myers said, expertly pulling out documents from the drawer of her desk.

Mr. Easton handed the leash to Mr. Creelman and sat down to fill out the forms.

"Thank you," Trevor said to Mr. Creelman.

"For what?" he demanded, knitting his bushy white brows together.

"For everything," Trevor said.

Mr. Creelman kept scowling, but he reached down and patted Buster. Then he slowly straightened and handed the leash to Trevor.

"I have to get back to the cemetery," he declared to everyone in the room. "I have a bone to pick with a bagpipe player who insists on practicing at the cemetery so loud, it's enough to wake the dead."

Mr. Easton turned around in his chair when he heard that.

"Will you be at Twillingate this weekend? I'll drop off the book you lent me," he said.

"I'll be there," Mr. Creelman said gravely. Halfway out the door, he turned and briefly nodded at Trevor before continuing on his way.

"What book did he lend you?" Trevor asked Mr. Easton.

"Famous Last Words," Mr. Easton said, turning back to his paperwork.

"The book with the epitaphs?" Trevor asked. "The one he read to us at the Queensview Mystery Book Club?"

"That's the one," Mr. Easton said, filling in the blanks, Buster lying at his feet. "I especially liked the epitaph about the fire-station mascot."

"Oh! I know it," Isabelle Myers said. She paused before reciting. *"The spotted dog last seen ..."*

"Patrolling ladders touching skies," Trevor continued.

"Now rests beneath the green," Loyola chimed in.

"And our tapestry of sighs," Mr. Easton finished.

Everyone smiled, including Buster.

"Oh! I almost forgot! I have something for Buster," Trevor said.

He dug into his knapsack and pulled out the stuffed toy ladybug, which was jammed against the book that he had bought for Loyola.

Buster stood up and wagged his tail. Trevor handed the toy to him. Buster gently set the toy between his two front paws as he lay back down beside Mr. Easton.

It was such a nice moment that Trevor wondered if he should give Loyola the book. He was beginning to slide his hand into his knapsack when she spoke.

"Well, I better get going, too. I still have to complete the last assignment for tomorrow's time-capsule ceremony. Thank you so much for everything," she said to Isabelle Myers.

"Thank *you*," Isabelle Myers said. "You both did such a good job that we've decided to run the program again next year. I hope I get two more students who are as responsible as you."

Loyola left, the bell ringing behind her. Trevor might have chased after her if he had not been holding Buster's leash.

Instead, he stayed put while Mr. Easton signed the last of the papers.

"All set?" Trevor asked as he handed the leash to Mr. Easton.

"You bet," Mr. Easton said. "I'll just need to drop by the grocery store for some dog food on the way home."

The grocery store was the opposite way from where Trevor lived, so he replied, "See you tomorrow."

He walked about a half a block, then stopped and did something he never did.

He looked back.

Mr. Easton was walking away, an extra spring in his step. Buster bounced along, wagging his tail nonstop and looking up at Mr. Easton from time to time.

Trevor let out the biggest sigh of his life.

It was the last day of school. Trevor woke up to a bright but empty bedroom. Everything had been packed, except for his bed. Even the curtains were gone. His room no longer felt like home.

His dad opened the door and poked his head in.

"Time to fly," he said.

Trevor flung back his covers and followed his dad downstairs where his mom sat drinking coffee from a paper cup in the bare kitchen with the emptied-out fridge.

"Breakfast on the go," his dad said, pushing a brown bag toward Trevor.

Trevor opened the bag. Inside was a warm egg and sausage sandwich, a banana muffin and a bottle of apple juice. He took out the food and flattened the bag to use as a plate because the dishes were packed, too. Tonight, he knew, they would go out for dinner, probably Trevor's choice, and then they would head straight to the airport for a late night flight. But before that, before they left for good, he still had one more day at school. That day included the time-capsule ceremony. And he still had no idea what he'd leave behind in the locker besides his last assignment, now that all his belongings were boxed up.

On his way to school, Miller joined him.

"I saw Mr. Easton last night," Miller reported. "At the soccer field. He was playing fetch with a dog."

"I know," Trevor said. "Loyola and I were at the animal shelter when he adopted it."

"He told me it was the same stray dog that was hanging around the school these past few weeks," Miller continued.

"Buster," Trevor confirmed.

They walked side by side for another block before Miller spoke again.

"I had to say goodbye to everyone at the used clothes depot," Miller said. "It was hard," he admitted. "I'm not very good at it, at saying goodbye."

"Not many are," Trevor said, feeling the weight of the book he had bought for Loyola still in his knapsack. But he liked how Miller had just told him goodbye without coming right out and saying it.

And then to change the subject to a happier topic, Trevor asked, "Did you complete the last assignment?"

"Yes. Got it in a sealed envelope and everything," Miller said. "It's awesome to think that no one will read our stories for fifty years."

"Wait up!" Craig called from behind them. He stopped to sneeze three times before joining Trevor and Miller. "Did Miller tell you about Mr. Easton's new dog?"

"Yes. I bet the whole Queensview Mystery Book Club knows by now!" Trevor said.

Bertram joined them as they headed up to the second floor.

"Do you have your last assignment?" Trevor asked.

"Yes. Mine's a poem," Bertram said. "An epic ballad."

"I'll bet," Craig said. He sneezed again.

Trevor undid his combination lock and put his knapsack in his locker one last time. He had already emptied out the rest of the locker in preparation for turning it into a time capsule.

As they entered the classroom, Trevor spied a note on the front board, written in Mr. Easton's loopy, backwards, left-handed writing.

Time-capsule ceremony: 2:00 p.m.

Trevor scanned the room, which was practically empty. Mr. Easton wasn't there yet, but he saw Loyola at the back, sitting alone at her desk, slightly slouched, trying hard to reduce her height. The usual routine.

His heart started to thump harder because he realized that it might be a good time to give her the book, with no one around to tease them. He was about to rush out the door, back to his locker to retrieve the gift, but then more and more students started to file in, and his moment was lost. Trevor slid behind his desk. Would he get another chance?

"Good morning, everyone," Mr. Easton called out jovially as he strode into the room.

"Good morning, Mr. Easton," the class chimed back, everyone in an excited mood.

After the national anthem was played, with students standing at attention, and the end-of-year announcements were read by the principal over the scratchy intercom, Mr. Easton led them through the morning's lessons. Only he went easy on them, it being the last day and all. Mostly he handed back homework and reviewed some math problems for those who didn't do as well on their last test. Then he read out loud the final chapters of *The Science Fair Incident*.

Before long, it was lunch.

"I did not predict that ending," Noah said, when he sat down to join the group.

Everyone knew he was talking about *The Science Fair Incident*.

"That's what makes a good mystery," said Bertram. "You can't predict the ending."

"Kind of like real life," Miller said, digging into his pudding.

Everyone stopped eating to stare at him.

Trevor knew why. It was probably the most insightful observation that Miller had made all year.

Trevor half-listened to the conversation as it continued, but for once he did not feel like joining in. Instead, he was lost in his own thoughts. Some things he *could* predict, he thought wistfully. In his haste to make new friends, he was pretty sure he would lose track of this group of classmates, just like he had done at every other school, with only his yearbooks to turn to. There would be promises to write and even promises to visit, yet Trevor knew those types of promises were made to avoid saying goodbye altogether.

Saying goodbye was just part of life. Trevor knew that. Why would this be any different?

"I wonder if another teacher will keep the Queens-view Mystery Book Club going, now that Mr. Easton is leaving," Bertram said.

"Even if someone else does, it won't be the same," Craig said.

Trevor thought back to the club photo, where everyone sat in a circle on the soccer field reading books that Mr. Easton had recommended for each of them. He nodded, along with the others. No one could replace Mr. Easton.

Having finished his lunch, Trevor glanced around the room. He spotted Loyola and her group of chatties at one of the tables. He could hear her laughter from where he sat, despite the loud voices and the clatter of dishes and cutlery all around.

Trevor briefly wondered if now might be a good time to give his present to Loyola, but he quickly dismissed the idea. She was surrounded by the chatties, and there was no way he was about to infiltrate that group. He'd have to try to catch her alone.

But when?

The afternoon wore on, and Trevor spent most of it trying to figure out the best time to approach Loyola. He couldn't even seem to catch her eye. It was rather hopeless.

And then it was two o'clock. The time-capsule ceremony. Everyone grabbed their last assignment and headed out the door.

The entire school was crammed in the hallway, just outside the grade-six classroom, with only a tight half-circle of space around Trevor's locker. Someone had placed a small wood platform on the floor right in front of the locker, and that's where Mr. Easton and the principal stood. Across the hallway, in the music room, the school's band and the choir had assembled, ready to perform as part of the ceremony. There was also a photographer standing off to the side. Trevor recognized him from the yearbook photo day.

The principal brought everyone to attention with his booming voice. He called upon Mr. Easton to deliver a speech on behalf of the grade-six class.

Mr. Easton told the crowd he was honored to speak to them on the last day of school. He thanked everyone he had worked with during the year — the librarian, the janitors, the secretary and the other teachers who helped him along the way.

Then he talked about how hard it was to say farewell. He said that he was going to miss them even though it had only been a year, and he got a bit choky.

There was not a peep in the crowd. Mr. Easton continued with his speech.

He went on to say that every single person at Queensview was a leader, that everyone showed it in their actions every day — in acts of kindness around the school or on the playground that inspired other students and their teachers. Mr. Easton ended his speech by borrowing a phrase from Mr. Creelman's *Famous Last Words*. He said that everyone should take what they learned from Queensview Elementary and use that to build ladders so high, they could touch the sky.

Trevor knew what that meant — everyone had endless potential.

He also had a hard time trying not to cry. It felt like he was swallowing broken glass, and he was pretty sure everyone else in the audience felt the same way. He had never been so sad about leaving a place in his life. And he now knew why.

It was because of Mr. Easton.

It was because of the animal shelter's Pet Patrol program.

And it was because of Loyola.

It was Trevor's turn to say a few words. He stepped onto the platform. Still, only the front row could really see him, so Trevor used his extra loud voice.

"What I really want to do is to get everyone I like in the same place and then have no one leave. That would be great."

Trevor paused as the audience mulled this over.

"But it wouldn't work. Someone would leave. Someone always leaves. Usually, it's me. Then I have to say goodbye."

Some of the students closest to him nodded sadly.

"My parents are pilots," Trevor continued. "They fly around the world, and they often tell me about having a perfect view of the curve of earth in the cockpit. They also tell me this — whenever you leave a place, if you keep going, eventually you will return to the exact spot you started. You never truly leave. So even though we can't stay together, this time capsule will hold a part of each and every one of us in the same place, a special place that we will never truly leave. See you in fifty years."

There was a heavy silence. Some students wiped at their eyes, and then the audience broke into wild applause. Mr. Easton gave Trevor a hug.

After the crowd settled, Mr. Easton asked Trevor to unlock his locker. Trevor spun the combination.

Twenty-eight. Thirty-four. Eighteen.

He opened the door and removed his knapsack for the last time. The locker was now empty.

"Do you want to put anything of your own in the time capsule before the others add their last assignment?" Mr. Easton asked.

Even after weeks had gone by, giving Trevor plenty of time to think about what he could put into his locker, he still had drawn a complete blank. His knapsack was heavy at his feet. He looked down at it. It was then that he realized with deep regret that he wasn't going to give his gift to Loyola after all. As brave as he had been to give his speech, he knew he wasn't brave enough to let Loyola know how he really felt about her. Besides, she didn't think of him as a true friend, not really. They had shared some good times with the dogs. That was it. She, like all others, would forget about him and his magnificent speech, even before the summer was over.

So he reached into his knapsack, took out her book and slid it onto the top shelf of the locker.

"That's it?" Mr. Easton asked.

"That's it," Trevor said in a little voice.

And then he placed his last assignment, sealed in an envelope with Mr. Easton's name written on it in his best penmanship, on the bottom of the locker.

One by one, the others in grade six came forward and did the same, each story sealed in an envelope addressed to Mr. Easton. Loyola, who stood at the back of the crowd, was last. Only she didn't place her envelope on the top of the pile. She lifted the pile up and placed hers on the bottom as Trevor watched, confused.

She stood and turned to face the crowd. Everyone gathered had a clear view of her on the platform.

"Because we have so much in common — our love of dogs and solving puzzles and cheese sandwiches — I placed my envelope next to Trevor's," she announced in the loudest voice he had ever heard her speak. It rang out beautifully to match her infectious laughter.

Just like that, Loyola had taken the first bold step to declare their friendship in front of the entire school. And no one had a word to say about it as she proudly made her way to the back of the crowd.

"Now the plaque," the principal declared.

Trevor shut the door to the locker and spun the dial on the lock. He pulled on the hasp. Locked. Mr. Easton stuck the plaque to the door. On it was Trevor's name, the year of their graduation and the year that the time capsule was to be reopened.

There was more applause along with hoots and cheers. Then the band fired up. They played an old-time song called "Hello, Goodbye!" and the choir sang along in rounds. During the final chorus, everyone in the audience clapped and stomped to the beat.

And then that was it. The ceremony was over. The crowd started to break up and drift back to their classrooms for final dismissal.

"Well done," Mr. Easton said, putting his arm around Trevor and steering him back to class.

Trevor should have felt great after the speech he had given, but he felt worse than worse. He should have given his gift to Loyola after all. Now it was locked away in the time capsule, practically forever. Any minute, the final bell would ring! And she'd be gone!

He slid behind his desk feeling numb. He barely heard the whoops and cheers when the bell rang moments later. He drifted with the crowd of merrymakers down the stairs and out the front door of the school. He barely took in who was saying goodbye to him as they swept past.

"Peace," Bertram said.

"Farewell," Noah said.

"Later," Miller said.

And Craig just fondly waved, too stuffed up for words.

Trevor plunked down on the steps, trying to pull his thoughts together as the school cleared out of teachers and students alike.

The crowd thinned.

Then there was just a trickle coming out the door.

Trevor was alone.

Not quite.

Someone sat down beside him, a giant bag filled with the contents of her locker slung over her shoulder.

Loyola.

"What did you write about in your last assignment?" she asked in her bold new voice that said, "I'm tall. So what?"

"We're not supposed to tell, are we?" he asked, his confused thoughts running every which way.

"I'll tell you if you tell me," Loyola said in her new-found voice.

"Buster," Trevor admitted.

"Me, too!" she exclaimed. "And like Mr. Easton said, I do feel better now that I've written it all down. I think things will work out for everyone."

"Me, too," he echoed, starting to realize that it was true.

"Which way are you going?" she asked.

"That way," Trevor pointed in the direction of his home, which was not his home anymore, not after today.

"Me, too," she said. "Want to walk together?"

Walk together? thought Trevor. *Without dogs or other distractions?*

He slowly nodded.

"Time to fly," she said. She got up with her bag.

Trevor stood, too. He was thrilled. Thrilled to be walking with Loyola.

No dogs. Just him.

They chatted as they strolled along the sidewalk. Mostly they talked about the funny things that Duncan had done, or Scout or MacPherson. When they got past the yawning iron gate of the Twillingate Cemetery, Loyola stopped short.

"I go this way now," she said, pointing to a street that intersected the one that they were on, the one that would lead her home. "I know you like hellos more than goodbyes," she added, her voice trailing away.

Trevor cut her off. He stood tall, stepped forward and gave her a really big hug.

She hugged back, then turned to go.

"Wait," Trevor said.

She paused.

He reached into his knapsack and pulled out his notepad and a pen. He tore off a sheet of paper and wrote down three numbers.

Twenty-eight. Thirty-four. Eighteen.

He handed her the paper.

"What's this?" she asked.

Trevor knew she'd figure out that it was the combination lock to his time capsule. He knew she'd make her way back to the school over the summer and open the locker. She'd find the book of codes he had left on the top shelf, and she'd know it was for her because she'd remember that she had told him about how much she liked solving puzzles.

Friends knew these things about each other.

"It's a mystery," Trevor said, and he grinned. "It's something I'm leaving for you to figure out. From one Queensview Mystery Book Club member to another."

Loyola nodded slowly, but she wore a beautiful smile.

And so they parted as friends without having to say goodbye at all.

Afterword

WHEN WE lived in the countryside near Peggy's Cove, Nova Scotia, we owned a dog named Astro. She was a nutty English springer spaniel who was full of beans and who would get lost in the woods from time to time when we took her out with friends on long hikes. We'd call and call until our voices were hoarse and night would fall, and we'd have to come home alone with our burned-out flashlights.

The worrying was relentless. What if she was hungry? What if she hurt herself? What if she came up against a bear?

Yet Astro would always find her way home by the morning, delighted by her midnight adventure but a little bit sheepish and grateful for her cozy bed.

Astro lived to be a happy old dog. Even after all these years, we still have her portrait on our family-room wall and her leash in our front porch.

Dogs, and other pets we love dearly, sometimes have to leave us. But they never truly leave. And if you ever need proof, just ask someone you know about a dog that they used to own. They'll tell you a story or two about cherished moments, and then suddenly during the telling of the story, they'll catch a fleeting glimpse — their missing dog now spotted — however briefly, but forever safe in their hearts.

Thank you to Sheila Barry and the exceptional staff at Groundwood for supporting my efforts to extend *The Spotted Dog Last Seen* into this prequel. Thank you also to Katie, Pepper, Jody, Maggie, Myles, Lark, Tiger, Dudley, Balto and Dougall, all good dogs, and to their owners who loved them.

About the Author

JESSICA SCOTT KERRIN is the author of the popular Lobster Chronicles series and the bestselling Martin Bridge series. Her novel *The Spotted Dog Last Seen* was a finalist for the Canadian Library Association Book of the Year for Children Award and the John Spray Mystery Award. It was also selected as a New York Public Library Book for Reading and Sharing.

Born and raised in Alberta, Jessica now lives in Halifax, Nova Scotia, and once owned a nutty English springer spaniel who inspired this book.